I0762481

MUÑECA

ALSO BY CYNTHIA GÓMEZ

The Nightmare Box and Other Stories

MUÑECA

Cynthia Gómez

G. P. PUTNAM'S SONS
NEW YORK

PUTNAM
— EST. 1838 —

G. P. Putnam's Sons
Publishers Since 1838
An imprint of Penguin Random House LLC
1745 Broadway, New York, NY 10019
penguinrandomhouse.com

Title page illustration by vgorbash/Adobe Stock

LIBRARY OF CONGRESS CATALOGING-IN-PUBLICATION DATA

Names: Gómez, Cynthia (fiction writer) author
Title: Muñeca / Cynthia Gómez.
Description: New York: G. P. Putnam's Sons, [2026]
Identifiers: LCCN 2025042266 (print) | LCCN 2025042267 (ebook) |
ISBN 9798217047574 hardcover | ISBN 9798217047581 ebook
Subjects: LCGFT: Fiction | Witch fiction | Romance fiction | Queer fiction | Novellas
Classification: LCC PS3607.O4877 M86 2026 (print) | LCC PS3607.O4877 (ebook)
LC record available at https://lccn.loc.gov/2025042266
LC ebook record available at https://lccn.loc.gov/2025042267

Printed in the United States of America
1st Printing

The authorized representative in the EU for product safety and compliance is Penguin Random House Ireland, Morrison Chambers, 32 Nassau Street, Dublin D02 YH68, Ireland, https://eu-contact.penguin.ie.

To the real people who let me borrow bits of you
for these pages.
And who let me borrow bits of you
to make up myself.

MUÑECA

INTRODUCTION

Never forget this, Natalia. To certain people, you will always be invisible. They won't see you. They won't see your gifts. That is not your problem, nor is it your excuse. Learn what your gifts and your talents are, and then use them to do some good. That's the best thing you can do with this one life you have."

The last time my mother said this to me she was forty years old and dying of cancer, in a hospital room with thick orange paint. I stole the water pitcher from her room after they sent her down to the basement. I don't know why; it's something I did a lot when I was a kid, until I got it under control. Mom would always find whatever I stole, no matter how far back I shoved it between the mattress and the box spring. As long as the objects were small and easily missed—a used typewriter ribbon, an old lipstick—she would just purse her lips and tell me to get back to my schoolwork. But in 1954 she started work at the Miramontes house and a week later she found one of their embroidered handkerchiefs in my bed. That day she gave me one of only two whippings I ever got from her, even though at ten I was closing in on her height.

"Natalia. You've always been more clever than that."

She was right, and I could neither understand nor explain my flashing urges to steal, the way my hands practically itched with the need to take something from that family, or, before them, from the office where she briefly worked as a secretary, or from the restaurant that routinely sat us near the kitchen and refused to refill our drinks. I was too young to make sense of it then.

Mom invented an excuse to clean the room the handkerchief came from, the enormous master bedroom overlooking the Orinda hills, where Mr. Miramontes sometimes slept with his wife. That night she came home and after she'd checked my sums and tucked me into bed she showed me: a single thread, plucked from the white lace. I tucked the thread in a jar and kept it, and if I close my eyes I can imagine it exactly: the tinge of rust on the lid, the crack in the cloudy glass.

Mom wondered out loud if my little thefts were because I was bored, and if maybe I needed more ways to use my talents and busy my hands. She brought home extra work from my teachers, especially thick packets of the math that I loved, where I could lose myself in columns of numbers, the pure triumph of finding square roots or memorizing endless digits of pi. The praises stacked up from my teachers, green ink at the top of my assignments and exams proclaiming me "clever" and "sharp." I was placed in the most difficult math classes, even getting special permission to take the bus to Oakland Tech so I could take advanced algebra in eighth grade.

It worked, sort of, mostly. But then as I grew taller and my body grew rounder, what came with it was something else, something restless and rattling, like a song in my head that I'd once known but forgotten. I started looking around me at the other girls at Tech, or at Casper's Hot Dogs, where I worked after school, and once I started to recognize the restless ones, like me, I couldn't stop noticing them. Girls who'd learned how to hide their restlessness, their hunger; who practically carried multiple selves in their purses. I might see them clipping dress pictures from bride magazines, their faces lighting up at the beautiful designs but going dark at talk of the groom. Or maybe going quiet, like me, whenever prom or homecoming came around and we were all supposed to find some boy's arm to attach ourselves to. Now I know what we all had in common, and it took meeting Doris to see it.

I met her in 1965, three years after high school, three years after my mother died. I was working as one of the "teller girls," what they called the human calculating machines who sat adding up bank deposits and making sure they all matched. The other two supervisors besides Doris were white ladies, but I don't remember their names. All three of them would roam the aisles in narrow skirts and high heels, and God help you if they pulled up your adding machine tape and found a single digit misplaced. Mine never were, of course, but I don't think that's why Doris noticed me. I noticed her too, and it wasn't just the teal skirts and pink pocketbooks and cat's-eye glasses she wore, or how much her deep brown skin seemed to glow. It was the way she carried herself. She didn't seem restless; she just seemed calm. As if whatever that song was, she was singing it inside her own head, true and clear.

One night she stopped me in the hallway, clicking her teeth

at my plain little pantsuit, and asked me if I wanted to come out with her and the girls. I was surprised when by "out" she meant "in." She took me to a building behind Swan's Market, a little apartment up two flights of stairs. Carla Thomas was on the record player and the high ceilings were thick with smoke and there were women everywhere, filling up the space. Standing at the bar cart, lounging on a green couch, two draped over each other in a chair, giggling into each other's ears. Doris hugged a woman in the kitchen doorway and they stood together, Doris saying something that sparked the two of them into laughter. And then they waved me over and her friend set a drink in my hand and then somebody was making space for me on the couch, and the women in the chair kissed each other in front of everyone, and right then something inside me melted, settled down. That rattling that I'd never been able to quiet, not even with those visits to my grandmother's dark little apartment, the shelves lined with spell books and sage and the spiders weaving away in the corner, waiting. I'd never heard that Carla Thomas song before, but in that room just then, I felt like I had been hearing it all my life. Even now if I sing it to myself ("A Woman's Love") I can feel that calm inside, gleaming and warm and smooth, like polished copper.

That night was the first step toward a life even my mother would be proud of, taking a room in Doris's apartment on Clay Street when her flatmate moved out. At first I thought Doris was trying to flirt with me, but she never messed around with roommates, she explained. I'd meet girls at house parties and sometimes at a semiunderground club called the Jubilee. At work I was just another invisible little brown girl in a little brown pantsuit, and that suited me fine. All of it suited me just fine.

That's the life I left behind to come here, Violeta, a life I won't endanger, even to help you. And if you could speak, you would tell me you know it.

ONE

The last time I was in this room it was shiny with tinsel and presents, the air blue with cigarette smoke. Now, in full daylight, both Mrs. Miramontes and her ivory wallpaper look like they've aged way more than six years. They're both faded and sprouting lines, and I think if Mr. Miramontes had had his way, they'd both have been replaced a long time ago. The calendar on the wall assures me it's May 1968, but everything else—the fading sofa, the damask curtains and their dangling threads—looks like it's been dormant for a hundred years. Even the warm air feels fast asleep.

I'm enjoying the itchy panic taking over her face when she realizes she doesn't remember me at all. I was the invisible girl who came to the house a few times a year to help out her mother, mostly for their big parties, the ones that shrank every year, along with their fortune. I guess being a parasitic landowner's not as lucrative as it used to be.

She recovers quickly, though: "You look so different, my dear. The years have agreed with you." I look basically the same as when I was eighteen, when I was last here, except that my hair's gone from a flip to a bun. But I smile and thank her, the way I'm supposed to.

"So do you have any real sense of what this job entails, dear? Many girls have found it too . . . taxing."

"Yes; I ran into one of your previous housekeepers at a party and we got to talking." I take a sip of tea, to busy my shaking hands. "She told me that your daughter is bedridden, and she needs constant care."

"That's correct, but I'm afraid it's more dire than that." Sorrow washes over her face, and I feel a tiny bit of sympathy for her. "Violeta was stricken three weeks after her honeymoon. From one day to the next she couldn't walk, couldn't talk, couldn't even sit up in her bed. She can breathe on her own, but nothing more." She takes a long sip of her tea, and I can see the sadness on her face, but, underneath that, a flash of fear. "The doctors have all been without a clue. She's been studied and poked and prodded and to what good? There she stays."

"I understand. I took care of my mother when she got sick, so I've done this sort of thing before."

I look straight into her eyes when I say this, something the help is not supposed to do.

"Yes, dear. I was so sorry about your mother. She was such a hard worker. So reliable and committed, unlike some of our girls." Girls. My mother was thirty-two when she came to this house, and forty years old when she died. After the funeral they sent me a bouquet of white roses and a card with sixty dollars inside—the equivalent of a week's pay. I threw everything straight into the trash and then after a few minutes I went back and rescued the bills.

"Thank you, ma'am. I was sorry to hear about your husband." I keep my face and my voice as neutral as I can. *Of course, I never heard that he died of a heart attack in Acapulco with his twentysomething girlfriend*, my blank face says. That detail stayed out of the papers, but the servants' grapevine has long tendrils when the gossip is that good. Mrs. Miramontes has to keep her expression as neutral as mine, but her teacup pauses a long time on its way to her mouth.

"That's very kind of you. And you won't feel lonely in this big old house? Only Sundays to go back to your . . . family?"

"I'll manage. This place brings back such memories." That's not a lie, exactly. I just didn't say what kind of memories they were. "And it's so good of you to keep Violeta at home with you."

"Thank you, dear." I can see she's not going to explain any further. There's something slightly off about her: Her eyes are a little too soft, her voice a fraction or two slower than it should be, like a record playing at 24½ rpm instead of 33⅓.

"Well, your references were glowing, and of course you know this house and how we like to do things. Perhaps now I should take you to see Violeta." Now it's my turn to fumble, spilling the rest of my tea on the tablecloth. I try to cover it up with chatter.

"Did Taleitha and Ruth-Anne both retire?" Taleitha started at this house before I was even born. I remember listening to her and my mother talk about bus boycotts and lunchroom sit-ins while I was pretending to scrub the silverware.

"Oh, I had to let them go years ago." This time it's her turn to grow clumsy, nearly dropping her teacup on the floor instead of the table. "But I must tell you that with those riots we saw last year I was so glad I did. I just wouldn't have felt safe otherwise. And then again with the horrors of last month. Such an undignified response to the loss of that poor man." She looks at me over her horn-rimmed little glasses, her face already expecting me to agree. And I have to say nothing and follow her up the stairs. As I get to the landing I see a torn piece of rug trying to curl up and out of the way, and I shove my boot in, hard, to tear it open even more.

"Well, here we are." She opens a room off the second-floor landing, a room I remember was saved for less-than-distinguished guests, with its tiny window and fading wallpaper.

"I'll leave you two to get acquainted." She doesn't even look into the room. I was wrong before; that sigh wasn't pity for her daughter, locked inside her own body forever, no way out. It was much simpler: Her only living child is defective. Violeta's not making babies or hosting parties or managing the crumbling house, so for these people, what good is she?

This room looks like someone set out to decorate purgatory and then got bored. Wallpaper the color of faded buttercups, a braided rug that used to be bright blue and green. A tiny window that looks out to a light well. A shelf with a set of Punch and Judy puppets, and a little-girl doll with blond pigtails. No pictures on the walls, no books for anyone to read to the body in the bed. So many things I can bring in to make Violeta's days better, to earn the gratitude I'm going to need if I want my plan to work. The radio is just babbling away to itself, some guy ranting about the scourge of the anti-war movement and the specter of women protesting in the streets instead of staying at home. I switch him off.

Her eyes widen when I come in, which of course they would, to take in a new visitor. They follow me as I pull up a chair to the side of the bed, piled with a thick comforter even in the afternoon heat. I haven't seen her eyes leave me once, and it looks like her chest is rising higher and faster than when I came in.

"I think you remember me. And I think you're in trouble. And I think I can help you get out."

TWO

There are men looking at me all over this house, painted eyebrows collecting dust along with their frames. General Mariano Vásquez Del Valle, Mrs. Miramontes's great-great-grandfather, watches me in his nineteenth-century gear as I slip into the kitchen and find a crystal bowl. His hands are gratefully receiving a land grant from the colonial government, the land this house still sits on. Some other ancestor stares down while I steal a pair of roses from a vase by the door. Another surveys his sprawling estate while I carry the bowl, filled with water, past his portrait glaring down at me from the stairs. A gray and tired-looking maid passes through the hallway below, and I duck out of sight just in time. I can't go losing this job before I've even been technically hired.

Inside Violeta's sickroom, I set a wooden tray over her still body and rest the bowl carefully on top. Then I whisper words over the water, words I haven't used in more than ten years, and I'm humming the bolero my grandmother sang when she taught me how to perform this test.

Violeta's mouth is trembling just a little and my hand starts shaking as I pick up the roses, and a few grains of pollen spill over the comforter. I take the first blossom, the petals fresh and pink and just beginning to unfurl, and I set it inside the bowl and tell Violeta to watch what they do.

Her eyes never leave the petals as the water soaks through them, and instead of floating they instantly shrivel up and die. I set the second rose in the water, and we both watch as it happens again, just like the first.

"I know why you're stuck in your bed. I know why you're stuck in your body. The doctors couldn't see it, because this won't show up on their tests. And they can't fix it, but I can." I try not to let the hunger creep into my voice, my hands already practically counting the bills. Or the thrill that this test actually worked, and that I'll be returning to a part of myself that for more than a decade has been hidden in a dark little box. A box my grandmother gave me, that I'll have to open again, with all its shining dangers waiting inside.

I take the wilted blossoms and hide them in a bowl of potpourri, with its horrible dead smell that reminds me of hospital rooms. Then I lean over to Violeta, close enough to smell the lavender soap they must bathe her with. My voice is soft and low, as if I don't want to frighten her.

"You can understand me, can't you? Blink once if you understand." Instead her eyes begin fluttering madly around, in a pattern that reminds me of a bird frantically trying to escape its cage. Then a heavy smell rises over the sweetness of the soap. Old leather, mustache cream, aftershave. I turn and follow Violeta's eyes behind me, to the door.

"I see you've met my wife."

The last time I saw Violeta, my senior year of high school, she was twenty-one, glowing in a baby-blue dress, spinning around the parlor on the arm of the man whose diamond glowed on her finger: Señor Andrés Guzmán de Torrijos. He was maybe forty years old and fresh out of Cuba, having fled Castro with a bank account full of cash but no land, sniffing out Violeta's family—land-rich, cash-poor—the way a shark smells fresh blood. The lights from the Christmas tree glowed green on his face as the two of them swayed to the tune of "Perfidia." Violeta looked like her body was there but nothing else, and her eyes kept glancing over everything but landing nowhere. Until they caught mine, and for a second I could read the expression inside: trapped, sad, those black eyes wide in her white face. The face that's now almost as pale as her bedsheets, as Andrés steps over to her bed. He introduces himself, his Cuban accent draped over his English like lace over a chair, kissing my hand. If he recognizes me—why would he?—he gives no sign anywhere.

"Did my mother-in-law warn you of the difficulties of this job? Almost none of the girls last very long." That's no surprise if Andrés looks at them all the way he's looking at me, like I'm a fresh young pheasant ready to be served on a plate.

"I'm used to hard work, sir. Tell me: She really can't communicate?"

"I've tried and tried, but unfortunately it all comes to nothing." Violeta's breathing is slowing now, eyes fluttering closed as if she's fighting off sleep.

"It's all right, my dear. Get your rest." There's a silver bracelet on her wrist, etched with floral designs. It stands out, bright and shining, especially when she's wearing no other jewelry. He strokes the silver now as he talks, as her eyes shut against him.

"She has nurses and others who come in—bathe her, do physical therapy, check her feeding tube, things of that nature—so your main role is just to be here. My mother-in-law is so busy with her charity work, and I have investments and concerns on several continents. For the most part it will be just you and Violeta, and of course she can't speak. So don't be surprised if you feel lonely sometimes in this big old house."

"Yes, sir. Thank you for your concern."

"It can feel very quiet at night," he continues, striding over to the far wall and opening a door to a narrow, windowless room, an iron-framed bed where I'll sleep, if I get this job. He runs his hands over the bedspread, and I turn my face to the wallpaper so he can't see me recoil.

"I'm sorry your room is so small. This house was built in the 1860s, in the days of ladies' maids sleeping right next door. But Violeta's on one side of your wall, and my study is right on the other." He smiles down at me, wolflike. "Please shout if you need anything. Even if it's late."

And with another appraising glance he's gone, shutting the door with a click. As if the click was some kind of spell, her eyes snap open and I lean down again, close to her face.

"I'm going to ask you some questions, Violeta, and you answer with one blink for yes, two for no. First: Do you remember me?" I know she saw me, that night of the Christmas party, but that was a long time ago. She was hardly ever here when she was growing up, always away at boarding school. I wonder what it was like to only come to this place for holidays and vacations, to feel like a visitor in her own house.

She blinks slowly at me through her thick eyelashes: *Yes.*

"Does your husband know you can communicate?"

Two blinks, one quick after the other: *No.*

"Is he dangerous?"

Yes.

"Understood. So those flowers? They were my test. They wilted because you're under a spell." I pause, to let her take this all in.

"I came here to help break it. And I want you to help me in return."

One quick blink: *Yes.*

"Wait—first let me tell you about your end of the deal."

No.

"So you're just agreeing? Just like that?"

Yes.

"Are you sure about that?"

Yes.

I take in the faded yellow buttercups, the blandness of this room. "Something tells me I shouldn't let your mother suspect why I'm really here. Am I wrong?"

After a long breath: *No.*

"So should anybody else know that you can communicate?"

No.

My pulse jumps in my throat.

"I have to . . . I need to take care of a few loose ends at home. Figure out a way to take a leave from my job, things like that." I think of my little desk at the bank, one of dozens in long rows, the endless ticking of the overhead clock and the *click-click* of the adding machines. As I stare at Violeta's trapped body they all vanish from my mind like smoke.

"I'm going to tell your mother I'm taking this job. I'll be back soon, and we can begin." I stop, looking at her still form, nothing to do but lie here and wait. "Three days. I'll be back in three days."

Her eyes never leave me, and I can't help it; I reach out and move a lock of hair off her face. I know it's not possible, but when I see her lips trembling I imagine they're trying to form a shape they once knew, a shape she used to perform on command. I imagine she's trying to smile.

THREE

"Wait a minute, Nati. Your grandmother was a what?" I can hear in Doris's voice every bit of the disapproval she's trying so hard to shove down. And underneath that, a tiny bit of fear.

"Still is, at least as far as I know. I haven't talked to her in years." My hand finds its way, a well-practiced move, to the scar tissue at my waist. "Can you hold the stepladder?"

Doris doesn't want to do any such thing. I can see it in the way her eyes keep landing everywhere but on my face. But she puts her manicured hands on the ladder so I can reach the top shelf of my closet for a box I know is there, somewhere.

"How come you never mentioned any of this before?" *Like maybe before I let you move in here*, I can practically hear Doris thinking. "Does this mean you can go to Grandma's house and she'll just whip up a spell for you? Can you ask her for something I can slip my boss, so he'll finally give me my promotion?"

"I'm not going back there. Ever."

"But you've been keeping her witchy stuff here all this time?" Doris asks.

"Nobody really calls it that. She'd just say she was good at spells." A spider crawls out of the corner, and I look down at the floor to steady myself.

"And are you good at spells too, Nati?" Her voice sounds like I've just pulled away my usual face and am talking to her from the new one underneath.

"I was learning. I stopped." *I got pretty good for a beginner,* I manage not to add. When I was thirteen I swore I would shut this box forever. I break that promise once a year or so, sometimes even touching the things inside, or running through the spells in my head, before reminding myself of that day with the shadows, and then back inside the box everything goes. Until now.

"So why start up again now?" Doris asks, pretending to steady the ladder. On the wall behind her is a free calendar from some travel agency, a year's worth of photos of places I could never afford to see. This month it's a beautiful redhead on a beach in Mallorca, her yellow sundress bright against the ocean, the sun on her skin. I point to it with my chin, and then to our hallway, the floorboards that won't meet, the light fixtures the landlord refuses to fix.

"Money. I'm going to free her and in return she's going to kick down some of her family's wealth. Enough for me to pick anywhere on that calendar and go. She said yes—I mean, she blinked it. Right away, no questions asked."

"Nati, of course she did. In her position, she's going to say no?"

I feel a stab of shame. "I'm helping her; why shouldn't she

help me? It's honest money; that's it. And I'm not even going there to cast spells. Just to break one."

You sure about that? her raised eyebrow seems to say. She's got a point, but this isn't the time to agree with her out loud. The only thing I need now is to find what seems determined to stay hidden in all this dust. I see boxes of winter sweaters, of my old report cards and my term papers that Mom always kept, but no metal canister that once held sugar cookies, way back in another lifetime. I keep sneezing, and the chain from the closet light keeps smacking me in the face.

The smell of roasting chile and tomato wafts down the hall from the kitchen, where a girl named Lupe is making enchiladas. Payment for letting her crash on the couch. There's always a rotating cast of couch girls, because there's no shortage of parents who stop being parents when they find out their daughter's queer. Lupe's one of my favorites so far; she's teaching us how to fix leaky faucets and dance cumbia. She pokes her head in the door now, wooden spoon in her hand: "Dinner's ready soon. You guys still coming to the White Horse later?"

Doris rolls her eyes. "Um, last time you dragged us there, we were supposed to be taking tequila shots and flirting with girls. And instead we ended up in their back room for some anti-war poster-making party—"

"And still flirting with girls," Lupe says, grinning. "You coming or not?"

"Don't be surprised if Nati bows out," Doris says. "She has to pack." And with a quick unreadable glance at me she's following Lupe down the hall. I'd bet money that when I get back in a few days I'll come home to some meeting / consciousness-raising session / flirt session in the living room, everyone eating tamales and listening to Aretha demanding her respect.

I hear them chattering in the kitchen, with its creaking cupboards and faded linoleum, Doris asking about some "cute little friend" of Lupe's who's maybe going to be there. I don't have to leave all this. I could listen to the nagging doubts I've been trying to calm since making my plan: What if somebody finds out what I'm doing, what if I've lost all my skill and can't get it back, what if magic is less like a force I can wield and more like a god, capricious and easily offended at being left behind for so long? I could call up Mrs. Miramontes and tell her I can't start work tomorrow after all. I could stay here, in this life that's always felt good enough.

Until two weeks ago. When I sat next to a woman at a party who'd just been fired by Mrs. Miramontes and had a very gossipy story to tell, straight out of a fairy tale: a beautiful damsel inexplicably locked inside her own body, a mystery nobody could solve. And somehow I knew, just knew, why nobody had been able to solve it, and I knew that I could. The plan practically began weaving itself: Get a job at the family's home, free the damsel from her spell, collect a handsome reward. Every time I've tried to shove the plan aside, it leaps back, doubts or no doubts, tugging at me with a pull like my own personal gravity, a force I haven't felt since the last time I saw my grandmother. I'd had good reasons for putting that box away, but I have better reasons for picking it up again now, a chance to help someone and be helped in return. I know what Doris would ask:

And are they good enough reasons to play with something so dangerous?

Now the light bulb flickers off, leaving me in the dusty dark. When it sputters back on, I see the box, shoved behind a pair of saddle shoes. The dust covering it almost seems to glow in the thin light.

FOUR

Undoing a spell is a lot harder than casting it in the first place, little girl. That's why you should think carefully before you cast one." I was a few months past thirteen and sitting at my grandmother's feet—literally; I could see the lace of her sneaker coming undone—while she tricked a spider into strangling itself in its own web.

"Why'd you do that?"

"That is the most boring question in the world." My mouth went slack to hear someone really talk that way, as if she'd grown up in some parallel world hiding inside and next to my own. I'd been raised with endless questions, all the time: *Who will be helped if you do this? Who will be hurt? Is there another solution?* And my constant companion, the one that I'd been trained so often to ask that it sprang up on its own now, unprompted: *Why?* And here was Grandma, tossing that question aside the way I did when I opened a cookie and read a fortune I didn't like.

I was somewhere I definitely was not supposed to be: Grandma's apartment on Adeline Street. I'd told my mother I was going to meet a classmate at the library, and then I'd got on the number 43 bus with a stolen address clutched in my hand. Grandma's place was thick with smells, of burning candles and crushed sage and the pot simmering on the stove. "Not witches' brew," she told me when I asked. "Just ordinary soup. Campbell's. I save my time for other things." Like asphyxiating arachnids. I stared at the swinging body, mesmerized by this parallel world that apparently had been waiting for me this whole time, just a bus ride across town.

We were in the tiny room off the kitchen that most people call a dining room. Sheets were nailed over the mold-frosted windows, and the room was thick with the dark and the damp. The built-in cabinet overflowed with books in two languages, pages yellowed and curling; conch shells, half abalone glittering with mother-of-pearl and dusted with crushed marigolds; bundles of herbs tied together with ribbons the color of blood.

"What's in here?" I stood and crossed over to a mirrored medicine cabinet on the wall, the paint a pale, sickly green. When I touched the glass knob a shock ran all through my body, knocking me onto the floor. Grandma laughed.

"That's your first lesson, little girl."

"What—how to electrocute your granddaughter?" The fall had been so sudden I'd bitten my lip, and flecks of blood wet my lips as I talked.

"No. How to keep your most important things secret. That cabinet won't open for anybody but me."

If I'd been a different kid, I'd have smiled and nodded and said some version of, "Sure, Grandma." Or I'd have invented some excuse to get the hell out of there. But I'd grown up surrounded by dark, swirling rumors about this woman. I'd noticed the way my mother changed the subject if anyone talked about magic or witchcraft, a topic she never brought up, even once. And I'd seen the ragged scar on her shoulder that she never spoke of, never explained. Grandma was another topic that my mother refused to touch, and I respected that bright red line my entire life, until I didn't. Until I turned thirteen and the lure of that secret was too powerful to ignore, the thought that Grandma's magic might be in my veins, waiting to bloom.

So when Grandma asked me, "Got any blood left?" and held a metal bowl under my chin, I hesitated only a breath before I spit into it, and then I watched as she opened a drawer full of twisted nails and rattling keys. "Choose." I picked the longest and most beautiful, a skeleton key tied with black ribbon. She rattled it into the bowl, swirled the key through the few drops that lay at the bottom, dampening the black with my blood.

Now she poured something else into the bowl, something acrid-smelling and dark. "That's just paint. See the label?" And then she stirred the whole thing together with the tip of a paintbrush and held the brush out to me. The mixture glistened black on the end of the bristles, ready to fall.

What she handed me then was an ordinary metal tin, dented and yellow, "Mother's Cookies" stenciled on the front. I wanted to laugh, but those eyes were boring into me, so I choked it off. "Nobody can open this but you," she said, once I had covered every bit of the bright yellow with black paint.

Sun filtered through the curtains in the kitchen—neat, tidy, no spiders in sight—while she served me a bowl of Campbell's and we waited for the tin to dry. The tin painted in shining liquid spiked with my blood.

It's the tin I'm opening now, sitting on the musty bedspread in the little maid's room, while Violeta sleeps on the other side of the wall. There's a small white bone, from what Grandma assured me is a real human hand, that I can use to make someone feel scratching up their spine, wherever they are, preferably when they're vulnerable, when they're alone. Harmless, really. There's a needle and thread that I buried in layers of foam and kept for weeks on the top shelf of the History Room at the library, where it could soak up the quiet. Give me a photograph of anyone and I can stitch their lips into silence forever. Or, at least, until I unweave the thread.

I pull out a stack of little cards, like the ones women use to write down recipes. There's a spell for making the victim dance and dance whenever a certain song plays; another one for staining their hands and their lips cherry red (or any color in the food coloring kit, really, but red is the most menacing). At the bottom is a paper sack of cheap jewelry: bracelets, dead watches, gaudy rings. They're some of the most dangerous things in this box.

I dangle a slim fake-gold bracelet between the fingers of my left hand. If I wanted to cast a spell that's nearly impossible to break, I'd first cast it into this bracelet. Then I'd give it to my victim, maybe slip it over their wrist while they slept, if I could manage that without waking them. Any piece of jewelry would do (though earrings are not a good choice: too prone to falling off). Sixty minutes to cast, sixty minutes to set. Easy. After that, the victim could take off the metal, leave it in a drawer for years, give it away, and the spell would keep its hold. Even if they began to suspect, if they sliced it into pieces with a bolt cutter, cast it into a flame, it wouldn't matter. Destroying it wouldn't help, and it wouldn't even be necessary. Only a witch—sorry, Grandma—would know what to do before even touching the cursed metal.

I have a very good idea of what went into the spell that's kept Violeta frozen and trapped inside herself, the spell that I suspect was cast into the bracelet she wears on her wrist. When it's time to break that spell, those are the steps I'll have to repeat. But in reverse. And tomorrow night, when everyone's asleep and I've gathered everything I need, that's exactly what I'm going to do.

FIVE

The house is as beautiful as it ever was, draped in damask and silk, ringed by pink English Rose bushes with their thickets of thorns. But the inside reminds me of a ghost ship. Only a few unlucky souls rattling inside. There are the two daily maids: Rosario, gray-haired, short, and round; and Fernanda, tall, dark, and quiet, somewhere around my age. And, of course, the nurses and physical therapists constantly floating into Violeta's room. The nurse this morning is shorter and darker than me, and when she speaks I recognize the Philippines in her voice.

"How long have you been here?" I venture, while I help her to change Violeta's bedsheets, the immobile body gripped in the little nurse's arms.

"I only started last week. I'm from an agency." She settles Violeta back in her bed, then starts to pack up her bag, shaking her head. "Such a beautiful girl. I tried to see if she can communicate. Some of my patients can. But nothing." I catch Violeta's eyes, just for a second, blinking at me behind the nurse's back, like Morse code, reminding me: *no.* Once the nurse leaves I take the mental ledger in my head and add more questions to the list, the one branching and doubling back on itself.

On Violeta's right wrist is that silver bracelet, with its floral designs. I remember the night of the Christmas party, helping my mother polish the silver tea set and asking her where Andrés's family money came from. "Sugar plantations, I heard," my mother said as she wiped away the dark streaks. "But it doesn't matter. I know what kind of people fled Castro. I know how much suffering built their wealth. This family too: There's misery in every beautiful thing in this house." The silver shone in her hands.

I reach out now and stroke the shining jewelry Violeta's wearing, this beautiful thing full of misery.

"Lovely bracelet. Did your husband give it to you?"

Yes.

"Right after your wedding?"

Yes.

"Why not your wedding ring, I wonder?" I see Violeta's eyes narrow a tiny bit, and it's the first time I've seen her say anything but yes or no. What other expressions have been waiting inside, while she's been lying here, rotting?

"Tonight. I'll explain more tonight." I don't mention that she's very likely been wearing her own destruction on her wrist for six years. "But first I'm going to make your life here a little more bearable."

I take a stash of mirrors from two of the unused guest rooms and hang them on every wall, reflecting each other, so she can see more of the room. Next, I pluck a fistful of gardenias from the front walkway and set them in a bowl of water on a dresser, right where Violeta's eyes go. I've got lilies too, but Violeta blinks her *no.* "Good job," I tell her, and throw them out the hallway window, into the garden outside. Finally, the wall clock, which I hang where she can see it, and the calendar I brought from home, where I cross out every day until today. Monday, May 13. The pretty girl in the dress smiles down at us both, the waters of Mallorca behind her, the sun glowing on her skin.

"Now we tackle the silence in this place," I tell Violeta. "It's like a funeral home." There again is that twitching at the corners of her mouth, the ghost of a smile. I unpack my portable record player, the first luxury I bought for myself, before even buying a real bed. It's a shiny pink, easily the most colorful thing in this room.

"You like Aretha Franklin, don't you?"

Yes.

I set the player next to her bed, and I gently, gently turn her head on its pillow, so she can see the needle as it slides through the grooves, the record as it spins and spins.

"I gave my friend Doris this album last year, for her thirtieth birthday." I smile at Violeta. "We dance to this in the kitchen sometimes." Violeta's nightgown is almost the same baby blue as that dress she was wearing that night, the last time I saw her dance. I hope there was dancing at her wedding, on her honeymoon. Those last few days of freedom, though she didn't know it then.

"Do you want to feel the music?"

Yes.

"May I take your hand?"

Yes.

I pick up her cold little hand and lay it against the side of the machine. I can feel the beat of her pulse, her blood thumping against my skin, speeding up as it feels the thump of the bass. Her face flushes in a way I haven't yet seen, her eyes wider and somehow more liquid than before, and staring directly into mine. It's so intense I have to look away, find the bag at my feet.

The front door slams, the sound echoing through the house, and then Andrés's boots thump into the hall, what sounds like suitcases dropping onto the floor. Back from some other trip, I'm guessing, some voyage to oversee his investments. I can hear Rosario rushing to tidy his rooms one more time, and Mrs. Miramontes ordering Fernanda to warm up something for him, her voice a bit too high-pitched, a bit too loud. Do his footsteps always send the women in this house scattering? Probably. I turn to Violeta, press my hand over hers.

"How about I read to you for a while?" I show her the book, the one I waited on for weeks on hold from the library. It's tucked inside a copy of *Rebecca*, ready if Andrés or anyone else bursts through the door.

So that's how we spend the rest of the morning, the sun bouncing off the mirrors and reflecting all through the room, the sweet smell of gardenias on the air, the music serenading us both as I read. I couldn't have picked a better album, a better meaning in this collection of songs. "A Change Is Gonna Come." "Save Me." I'll do it, Violeta. I will. The door stays peacefully shut and Aretha's voice climbs to heights I never knew a voice could reach, singing of freedom and hope, as I read to the body in the bed, from *The Autobiography of Malcolm X.*

SIX

The grandfather clock ticks its soft way toward midnight, and the house is quiet and still. I'm laying out everything I will need on the dresser next to Violeta's bed. First is a fistful of English Roses, and another bowl of water that I balance on her chest. Just like before, the first blossom turns brown as soon as it touches the water, but next is the real test. Before I toss in the second blossom, I take her bracelet and touch it to the side of the bowl, and again I whisper to the blossoms, "Show me."

In less than a second, less than a breath, the petals turn black and crisp. Violeta's eyes are wide and staring up at me, and I set the bowl on the table and explain what I knew, without thought, the moment I saw that thing on her wrist—what those blackened petals have confirmed.

"Listen, muñeca. That spell that's keeping you trapped in your body? It needs this bracelet right here. The one you told me your husband gave you. I had to test it, to be sure, and you just saw the results. I have to undo the spell before I even take it off of your wrist." I can see it in her eyes, the panic, then the fury, as she realizes what's been touching her skin all these years. I look straight into those eyes, letting her see the calm in my own, and I let her see me organizing my materials, smooth and confident, as if I were counting out a bank deposit by hand.

First a clean dry towel from the kitchen, then on top of it a bundle wrapped in white, sodden and cold. The needle scratches against the record, one I found in the parlor this morning, coated in a thin layer of dust. The Mills Brothers, singing about getting a paper doll to call their very own. Was this song playing while Violeta was turning into a doll in her own bed? *Una muñeca de piel*, my mother would say. Would have said. I play the record backward, the words and the melody a choppy gibberish, unspooling themselves in reverse.

Violeta watches me unwrap the wet white cloth from around a picture of her. It's from her wedding, her new husband's hands firmly gripping her waist. Fernanda caught me taking the picture from the sideboard, but I had a story prepared: "I want Miss Violeta to remember a time when she was happy." Fernanda's response was a single raised eyebrow, before she headed upstairs with a basket, ready to be filled with the family's dirty laundry.

I had to wait until the house was nearly empty, the help all gone for the day, Mrs. Miramontes off at some book club, before tearing Violeta's image away from her husband's side and setting it in a glass of water that I hid at the back of the freezer. It's only because I used no spells at all when I did it, steeped no herbs, played no music, that Violeta's not shivering now. The ice around her picture begins to melt in my warm hands, freeing her image, while the song sings itself back to the beginning. Before the men sang about a doll that would always be waiting for them at home. "I free you now, Violeta," I whisper, and her face emerges as the layers of ice melt away. "When I cut the spell's connection, you will no longer be frozen." When the ice is fully gone I set her damp picture in her cold little hand.

"Now I release you from your trap." I couldn't find mouse-traps in this house, but there were some in the fancy garage. Violeta's baby-blue convertible was there, covered in a dusty black shroud. No sign of Andrés's emerald-green Porsche, or Mrs. Miramontes's pearl Cadillac.

So I pry open the metal prongs of the trap I found, the one holding a stiff little mouse. It couldn't be helped; I needed to unspring a trap that had already been sprung. The little body tumbles into the wastebasket. The last thing I need to reverse the spell.

The metal eye of the bracelet opens wide in my hands. The chain drops to Violeta's chest, nestles onto her baby-blue gown. I pull it away, dangle it in front of her, loose and weak.

"Speak to me. Are you free?"

The answer doesn't come from her lips, the way it should. It comes from her eyes, just like before.

No.

SEVEN

Dreams and nightmares are dangerous things," Grandma told me on my first visit, after we'd had lunch. She opened a jar and a pair of teeth rattled into her molcajete. Tiny, pearly white. She reached for the pestle and began to grind them into a fine powder, her eyes locked on my face. "You can try to make a pretty little dream, but the line between dream and nightmare is as thin as that web." She pointed with her chin to the spider in the corner, the one I could imagine plotting revenge for the murder of its sister. "And the only way to find out is the hard way."

"They aren't your specialty, then?" This was a brand-new concept, the idea of my grandma like a chef known for her particular flavor of spells, and I was already wondering what mine would be. Maybe calling all the objects in a room to stand at attention, cleaning and ordering themselves. Maybe making the equations move all around on the blackboard in math class, forming new ones, or new symbols nobody had ever seen.

"No." She didn't say anything else, just spread a stinking salve into the bowl of the molcajete, swirling it together with the powder, and then she scraped the whole mix into a jar that had once held marmalade. A pair of feet rattled up the steps, and Grandma opened the door to a thin, plain-faced woman, who laid a twenty-dollar bill in Grandma's hand.

"This looks even stronger than last time." The woman's tone was approving but she was holding that jar as if whatever was inside might leap out through the lid.

"It'll bite harder this time too," Grandma said, grinning, and shut the door.

So after I've promised Violeta I'll keep trying, and I've let Chopin lull her into sleep, I begin weaving a dream for myself, Grandma's warning ringing in my ears. I use a handful of crushed violet petals, and a few of Violeta's nightgown threads, and the sodden picture freed from its icy cage.

I have no idea why my spell failed, or what to do next. Before I saw her in that bed, Violeta was no more than a story told to me in a dark room. An abstraction, something I could still walk away from. Now I know I can't. "I'm not going there to cast spells. Just to break one," I said not two days ago. *It's always dangerous when you start kidding yourself,* my mother would say.

This dream could tell me what I need to know, because spells speak the language of metaphor, the way dreams do, and sometimes the answers we need only speak in metaphor. But if I'm not careful, it could also become a nightmare that will follow me even when I'm awake. I might find myself in a nightmare of birds, like in that Hitchcock movie, and then I might wake up to see the shadow of their wings on the wall. Or look into a mirror to see their reflection gathering over my head. "Nightmares have no real rules," Grandma told me. "And bringing magic into them is like dragging your hand through a dark pond. You never know what you'll dredge up."

The clock ticks downstairs. I can feel the scratchy sheets against my face, the stale air lulling me into sleep.

I know I'm dreaming right away because the walls of Violeta's room are no longer the color of faded buttercups. Now they're baby blue, like her dress from the party, and hung with paintings that seem to shimmer and move. I'm standing over Violeta's bed, and she's tucked into the sheets, tight, like a straitjacket. The light through the window is going from daylight to darkness and back again. The spider is strangling itself over and over in its web. The bracelet is slipping from Violeta's wrist again and again, and the record player spins backward, achingly slow, so slow I want to smash it against the ground and scream. But when I lift up my hands, they're not my hands. My skin isn't my skin. I spread out my arms, two stiff things, smooth and pale pink. They're a doll's arms. Like the doll that sits on a shelf in Violeta's sickroom.

There's a silver bracelet on my left wrist, and I know the name engraved on it is mine, but when I try to read it, the words crawl around and I can't track them. There's an emerald-green scarf wrapped around the bracelet, and when I try to pull the scarf away, Violeta's wrist moves, and she moans from the next bed, and I follow the long trail of green to see that it's also wrapped around an identical band on her wrist. We're tied together. Almost bound.

~

When I wake in the dark I lie very still, then I run my hands over my own skin, warm and soft. I count all my fingers and toes, I'll admit it, and I silently recite prime numbers up to 113. I'm pretty sure I'm really awake; a dreaming mind would get bored and skip to the end.

I feel my narrow wrist, the tiny bones. Those twin bracelets, in the dream, were on both of our wrists, and both of them tied by the same tether. A scarf the color of emeralds. Or a gleaming Porsche, or the Christmas tree lights on Andrés's face.

Yes, dreams speak in metaphor, but poetry was never my favorite subject. Am I looking for an actual scarf in some shade of green? Or is the color a symbol, nothing more, of Andrés's blinding greed?

My doll hands, then, in the dream. My smooth plastic skin, pale as Violeta's, that pedigreed Spanish bloodline. My doll arms, moving stiffly, but moving.

When I understand I sit up so fast the bed squeaks, as if in complaint. I throw back the covers and step to Violeta's bed, where her black hair lies in ropes over her shoulders, two thick pigtails I made just this morning.

Her eyes flutter open at the sound of her name, wide as you would expect from someone just dredged from sleep.

"Everything's okay, muñeca," I murmur, the Spanish feeling rich on my tongue. I can understand it well enough, but speaking it usually makes me shy. Not now. I feel the rush of my blood again, the way it felt when I sat on this very bed and watched a rose blossom shrivel and die, and I knew there was a spell here, a spell I could break.

"I know you want to be free in your own body. And that will come." I try to make my voice sound more assured than it really is, to make sure she hears only the excitement I feel, and not the fear, at using the little card waiting inside that box. "But for now—for tonight—would you like to be a doll?"

EIGHT

It's now almost three in the morning, and I should not be doing this. If weaving that dream was a foolish step, what I'm doing now is an entire dance into madness. Even my grandmother didn't touch these kinds of spells. They were too unpredictable, she told me, slapping my hand away—not gently—when I dared so much as to pick up and read the card. The card I committed to memory the second her back was turned, and wrote down once I got home, my handwriting neat and tidy, even at thirteen. The one I'm casting now. So much for coming here only to break spells.

I don't know if I could explain to anyone else why I'm doing this, wandering further and further into this tunnel, the ground thin as a gossamer web under my feet. It's not just about the money, and maybe it never was.

The embroidered flowers of Violeta's bedspread are the same dark maroon as the hallway carpet downstairs. I once dropped an entire tray of wineglasses on that carpet, when I was twelve. Instantly, Mrs. Miramontes thundered down the stairs, hissing about my clumsiness. Violeta came out of the library, where she must have been quietly reading, and without a word she bent down to help me pick up the shards. Her hand grazed mine, just for an instant, a brush of silk on my skin. She didn't even acknowledge it, didn't look up. Mrs. Miramontes shifted gears real quick when she saw her daughter, murmuring something about being sure not to cut myself. When the pieces were collected Violeta went back to the library, quiet as she'd come.

The memory tugs at me now, just like the memory of that Christmas party, when I caught the distant, frightened look in her eyes. Even with that silk dress and gold necklace, she was trapped, just like she still is, right now. Trapped by the same man. Only this time, if I keep going down that gossamer path, I can find the way to get her out. And I'm the only one who can. How can I possibly give up now, knowing that?

Or maybe you just need an excuse, my grandmother would say. I push the thought away and open my hands, hot in the chilly air and tensing with anticipation. I'd forgotten how thrilling it feels, that mix of power and danger, a sensation that nothing else has rivaled, not in eleven years.

I turn to the little blond doll that I pulled down from the shelf. It's maybe a foot tall, with jointed limbs and eyes of glass, the same color as its baby-blue dress. I sit the doll across from Violeta and I start the first step of the spell, her eyes following my hands as I take hers, ready to begin. And then I feel a rush of shame. Everyone around here handles Violeta with no explanation. They treat her like . . . a doll. And I haven't been much better. So I start again, and with every step of the spell I ask if I can keep going, and I watch her eyes as they answer me. When I ask her permission for the very last step I have to stifle an awkward giggle, covering it with a cough. Her eyebrows look again like they're trying to furrow, and I can imagine her thinking, "Say what?" before she blinks *yes.*

And I don't know why—maybe it's just that we're already so far into the land of the absurd—but now I turn to the doll too, and I ask, "May I?" It's not one of those talking dolls, so I just move the pigtailed head so that it too nods *yes.*

Only then do I press its tiny, hard plastic lips against Violeta's, and try not to collapse at how bizarre, how silly this all feels. That all changes when I feel the doll move in my hands.

~

It's possible that this is not real. It's possible that I'm still tangled in the dream I wove a few hours ago. I should go get some water to splash on my face, the colder the better. But I don't want to be anywhere but right here, watching a little blond doll stretch out her pale plastic arms in front of her face. The round pink-painted mouth can't move, but the head can move up and down and swivel left and right. I set her on top of the dresser, facing the mirror, so she can see herself move: the slightly bent legs that move all of a piece; the little arms swiveling at the shoulder, the elbow; the hands molded into a shape resembling little fists, swiveling at the wrist. The blue eyes blinking and blinking, as if in utter disbelief.

She can walk, but stiffly, and constantly risking a fall; this doll was only made to be carried around, to be moved by someone else's hands. I extend my hand to her so she can use it as a kind of balance, a human walker, as she maneuvers across the dresser, back and forth. Finally, I place a Ouija set in front of her, which I stole from the family's parlor, and I put the planchette and board within her reach.

"What's your name?" I ask the little pigtailed head, just in case, and it tilts to the left as if I've said something ridiculous. Nonetheless, the planchette slides under her plastic hands. It's an awkward movement since the planchette is too big for the fists to grip, but she manages it, spooling the letters together like a chain: *Violeta.*

"And what's my name?"

The blue eyes blink, and blink, and then the planchette slides along. She spells my full name, the one I haven't told her, the one only my mom used with me: *Natalia.*

This is really her, then. A warmth spreads over my cheeks, down my neck.

"There are so many things I want to know, Violeta. I don't know where to start."

Her hands don't hesitate, moving from letter to letter like the needle dips over the record, the grooves crackling into a song.

My mother and my husband.

"Yes?" She's going to fill in the gaps of the story, the answers to the questions that have been filling up my mental ledger since I arrived. I look up at the door, firmly shut, and I hear the silence in the hall. I watch her hands speed through the letters, and my mouth opens wide as I read what she's spelling out.

Kill them.

NINE

"Grandma, have you ever killed anyone?"

My grandmother didn't change her expression, didn't blink. She just strolled over to her kitchen window and ran her hands over the herbs in little containers that crowded the sill. After a moment she pulled a sprig of peppermint from where it grew in a china teacup.

"I stole that cup from a Junior League meeting, when I was still a janitor. One of the coldest places I've ever been. Full of ladies in their fine dresses and pearls, ladies who didn't see me at all. Amazing, what I could have gotten away with, don't you think?" She crushed the peppermint in her hands.

"Look around you. This room is full of things that you can use for your own purposes, if you only learn how." She ran her hands over the ceramic teacup and along the crack on its side, over the bundles of dried herbs, through the shadow in the corner of the floor. "So is the whole world, if you look with the right eyes. Things just ready to be cracked open, for you to use what's inside." She reached over and plucked a long strand of my hair from my head. I didn't even gasp or cry out. I was mesmerized.

"To certain people, women like us are invisible." Now I knew where my mother had got that phrase, and I shivered. "Foolish of them, because then they won't see what's coming. It's fine with me if they want to relegate me to the shadows. Lots of dark and powerful things grow there." And she put my hair and the mint into her molcajete and mashed them together, eyes locked on mine.

"Hand me that jar of water in my fridge." She hadn't hypnotized me, not exactly, but in that moment there was nothing else I wanted to do but obey. I fetched the jar and I watched as she pulled a record from the cabinet on her living room wall, and she poured the cold water into her molcajete as a song began to play.

"You all right, little girl? You look a bit chilly." It was a warm day in April, but inside my chest it was now December, and growing colder with each breath.

"Grandma, what are you doing? What is this?" I said through trembling lips.

"This is a shivering spell. Now, peppermint works all right, but hibiscus is better, if you can find it. Dill works too, and chamomile. And if you can't steal something from a Junior League or some other cold place, try a cemetery at midnight. It's a cliché, but it works."

This was only my second visit, and I was pretty sure she wasn't planning to truly hurt me, not really, but I wouldn't have counted on that right then. I grabbed for her orange afghan, warm from the sun.

"That won't work. The cold is inside you. Don't worry; if I'd really wanted to do some damage I'd have steeped the herbs in ice water for days first, and I'd have the whole thing in the icebox. And I'd need more than just the one strand of hair. A photograph too, and some of your possessions. Especially anything that made you feel empty, and cold." Now she stopped and looked at me, and she began to play the record backward, and Buddy Clark sang in reverse, a series of choppy gibberish syllables that no longer sounded anything like "Baby, It's Cold Outside." And she whispered something to the mortar and pestle, and she pulled my hair out of the cold water, and inside my chest it grew warmer again. I'd wondered why my grandmother had so many records, such an odd variety of songs. Now I knew.

"You'll be fine in a few minutes, little girl. Definitely not going to develop a mysterious chill after getting a bad habit of hitting your wife and little daughters for being late with dinner. Definitely not going to develop pneumonia and die." And she rubbed her left ring finger, a place where I'd never seen a wedding ring, but now I could see a terribly faint indentation, where long ago a gold band might have been. I'd heard my mom and Tía Soledad refer to their father as a bully, but they'd never shared more, and I hadn't asked.

I kept looking back and forth, back and forth—between Grandma and the door and the living room table, where the painted cookie tin lay. And then beyond those, the room, and the house full of things my hands were already reaching for, things waiting to be cracked open, so I could use what was inside.

"The cup. Does it have to be stolen?" My voice was still shaking as the cold drained away.

She shook her head, a tiny smirk on her lips. "Probably not. But it feels good. And it doesn't have to be a teacup. You can grow a plant in all sorts of things. Now, someday you might meet someone who just needs to shiver themselves out of this world. So you take this card and write down what I told you."

I did, but on the bus ride home I stared and stared at that card, at my own handwriting, with its instructions for death. In the afternoon light and away from that place, those words repulsed me, and I took the card and tore it into tiny pieces and threw them out the window as the bus drove on. No use, of course, because as I close my eyes now I can see every one of those words, and hear every one of the steps she told me, clear and plain. And I can hear the story humming underneath those instructions, rattling inside me now as I sit by Violeta's bed, a blond doll and a Ouija board on the dresser next to me. The answer to the question I asked Grandma, an answer she gave in a story, but right there if I strung together the clues. The story of a husband who beat my grandmother, my mother, my aunt, and who one day had no idea why he was suddenly so terribly, terribly cold.

TEN

I watch Violeta's plastic fingers tracing over the planchette as the night creeps toward dawn. Hanging over both of us, unspoken, are the words she spelled out for me, the first real thing she's communicated in six years, the words I haven't responded to yet: *Kill them.*

Her dolly hands are clumsy, at first, but she gets the hang of it, stringing words together a letter at a time, and as each word forms I say it out loud. *He never loved me. He wanted the land. I inherited at 21. I didnt love him. Loved his attention. His promises. Fancy honeymoon. Hawaii. Milan. After h moon saw him w another woman. Women. Humiliated. Went to lawyer. Had to hire a PI.*

"Why'd you have to do that?"

Again the little blond head cocks to one side, as if I've said something ridiculous.

Needed proof. Otherwise judge wouldnt give divorce. Got proof. Also he was cheating to get loans. Lying on apps. Pretending he already owned my land. I remember that glimmering emerald scarf in my dream, the color of money, the color of blinding greed.

Cut him out of my will, filed for divorce. Gave papers to him myself. So stupid. Next morn woke up like that. And the pale doll's hand points to the living doll in the bed, temporarily stripped of its soul.

"Did he ever admit it? What he did to you?"

Bragged about it. When I came back from hospital. Said was best money he ever spent.

"He had no idea you could communicate."

No.

"And if he ever learned . . ." I need a breath, a moment, before I can make myself ask the rest of the question. But Violeta answers what I haven't yet asked: *He wont kill me. He needs me. But he could hurt me.* The night-light flickers a few times and in the shadows it casts, all kinds of dark things seem to twitch.

"And your mother?" But then I already know. "You tried to communicate with her. Didn't you." It's not a question.

Yes.

"And what happened?" The doll's arms are plastic; they can't tremble, exactly, but the next words are raggedy as they form.

She pretended not to see.

For a moment I don't even want to breathe. I don't want to take in another breath of the air in this house, thick with the silence that Mrs. Miramontes has covered herself in for six years, white and smothering.

Kill them, is what Violeta spelled out, the first time she could communicate anything. I let myself imagine those two ghouls, shivering from a chill that grows worse every second, coughing and desperately piling every blanket onto themselves. Ringing for a doctor who will never be able to save them, who will never think to check the freezer for a photograph wrapped in herbs and clouded with thickening ice. I imagine Andrés, trapped inside his own body while he feels invisible teeth biting their way along his flesh. I clasp my hands together, feeling the thrill rushing through them, the promise of power warm and humming, black streaks of fury running through. My lips are already shaping themselves to form *yes.*

"No." I say it quick, before my mouth can betray me. "No. I'm not killing anyone. I told you what kind of deal I was offering. I break the spell, I help you escape, you reward me, that's it." I'm saying this to myself as much as to her. "I'm not here for revenge."

The planchette slides over the board. *You sure?*

I don't dare answer that.

My face is red and flushed, my hands still throbbing with heat. I pull up the window sash and let the cold air flood through, and the movement slides my watch down my wrist. My mother's watch, really; a Citizen, cool on my hot skin. It's maybe what I needed to pull me back to myself, to this room, to remind me that I am twenty-four years old, not thirteen, no longer punch-drunk and fascinated and pulled like gravity toward something I can't fully control.

"Violeta. Even if I thought I could get away with it, that's not the only question to ask. I'm not dragging their ghosts around on my conscience the rest of my life." Though part of me wouldn't mind so much.

Then let me do it. The thought is so wonderful I clap my hand over my mouth, so the laughter can't escape. Andrés waking up to see a pale-faced doll looming over him in the moonlight, bearing a tiny blade. It actually hurts to make myself put the image away.

"And then what happens next, Violeta? After you kill Andrés in his bed? I'm supposed to tell the detectives that it wasn't me, of course not, even though I have no alibi. No, it was my patient, Violeta, summoned into a doll with pigtails." The little blond head sags. She knows I'm right.

"I didn't come here for that. When you're free you can do whatever you want to them, if you like."

Her plastic foot kicks at the planchette, and before I can stop her she's kicked it onto the floor, with a force I wouldn't have thought possible. "What the hell are you doing?" I hiss. "Are you trying to wake up the whole house?" Sure enough, a door creaks open down the hall.

"Did you forget how to think? You know nobody even bothers to knock on your door." I scramble for the planchette and tuck it and everything else under the comforter just as Andrés calls out, "Is everything all right in there?" I set her on the shelf by the door, and now the knob starts to turn.

"One move and I'm not helping you," I whisper into her plastic ear, and when the door opens Andrés finds me standing quiet and still, nothing in my hands.

His body fills up the doorframe, looking like something carved out of icicles and ebony. Pale blue eyes behind thick glasses, pale skin; then rich black hair, reflecting the overhead lights. His pajama pants are satin, like the dressing gown loosely thrown over his chest.

"Is everything all right, Nati?"

I'm shocked at the familiarity, but of course I can't show it.

"Yes, Señor Guzmán. I was just looking at your dolls and I dropped one on the floor." I shouldn't have said "dolls." His eyes flicker up to the shelf.

"They're nice, aren't they?" His hand reaches into the air. *Don't move,* I think furiously at the blond doll above my head. Above his. He picks up one half of the Punch and Judy set.

"I loved Punch and Judy when I was a boy." He lifts the strings up on Punch, and the wooden fingers stab the air, up and down, in front of the painted face. On the shelf, the pig-tailed doll's eyes begin to blink.

"Could I— Señor Guzmán, could you do that one move again? Just that—that one move?" I draw out the words as slowly as I dare, to remind Violeta of my warning: *One move and I'm not helping you.* He gives me a smile I'm sure he's used thousands of times before, and the wires dip and glide in the air. The blond doll sits very still.

"Thank you, sir. I'm so sorry to have woken you."

"Oh, you didn't wake me. I was packing; I have a flight in just a few hours. Zurich. Have you ever been?"

"Um, thank you for checking up on me. That was kind of you. I'm sure I'll sleep soundly now." That's as near as I'm allowed to get to just asking him to leave. He doesn't; instead he smiles up at the little blond doll on the shelf.

Oh, god; he's going to pick her up. *You don't get to touch her,* I want to scream. *You never touch her again.*

"This doll was a childhood toy of my wife's. Went with her to boarding school, I believe." He reaches up and strokes the flaxen hair. She doesn't react, doesn't blink.

"Do you like dolls, Nati?" He takes a half step closer to me.

So cool. *Butter wouldn't melt in his mouth*, my mother would have said. She also would have squeezed my hand, tight, and told me, "You can stand your ground with him, Natalia. I have confidence in you."

"Thank you again, sir. I'll sleep well now."

My chest loosens as his hand leaves the doll and he finally steps toward the door. "As always, let me know if you need anything." He slips a hand to the open folds of his dressing gown, scratching his chest, as though I'm not even here. In the dim light of the hallway I can see a silver chain, like a tiny rope, around his neck. And, dangling from the center of the chain, a silver bracelet. Exactly like the one Violeta wears on her wrist.

ELEVEN

It's the early hours of Tuesday morning, nearly dawn, and I don't want to put Violeta back in her body. I don't want to take away this narrow slice of freedom she's had, however imperfect and small. I don't want to put that horrid silver thing back on her wrist. But I have to, and so I promise her, "You can be a doll again tomorrow, and again every night I can manage it, until I free you. For now I need rest. I'm no good to anyone like this. I'll get a few hours of sleep and then I can—we can—think about what to do." I'm so tired my voice sounds like I'm pouring it through a strainer. And the dolly head nods and then I press the plastic lips against Violeta's sleeping mouth, and then the doll is only a doll again, and Violeta is back inside her body, eyes wide and alive.

"Do you remember tonight? All of it?"

Yes.

"So you remember me telling you that if you pull something like that again, I'm leaving?"

Yes.

"I won't kill anyone. And I can't draw any attention. Your mother clearly doesn't care about firing people. You've seen how many girls come and go. And we both know how bad it could be if Andrés even suspected what I'm doing here. That's why I had to put that thing back on your wrist. We can't have anyone wondering why it's gone. We have to be clever about this. Understood?"

She responds right away, blinking *yes.* But if I were in her place, I'd promise anything right now. Later I'd worry about whether I could keep it.

"Look, I came here because I knew I could help you, and helping people is something I was raised to do. But there are things I won't risk. I have a life that I've built, Violeta, and people I love." I see her eyes flicker away at that, and I smile. And even though I'm wrung out with exhaustion I settle into the chair again, and I tell her what I haven't yet. About the handkerchief I stole, the thread I still keep, and why I keep it. About meeting Doris, about the party she took me to and the door it opened to the life I left back at home, the one I want to go back to, when all this is done.

When I ask Violeta again if she understands, her blink is slower, more certain, her eyes fixed on me. And the need wells up inside me, my hands open and ready to touch her face, to touch her anywhere, to mark the agreement we've forged together, that slender and dangerous thing. And just like that first day, I pull a stray lock of hair away from her face, and my fingertips graze her cheek. I see her heartbeat jump in her neck and I wonder what it would feel like to press my fingers to that spot, to feel her pulse beating against mine.

I open the door to my windowless room, and the second I touch the rough sheets I fall right into a dream. My skin is made of violet and rose petals, and they slough off in glimmering piles whenever I move. My grandmother points to the cookie tin, tells me the spell I need is inside. But all I find is a set of Russian dolls, with pale skin and black hair and a baby-blue gown. My hands are finally pulling open the last one when I hear Rosario clattering on the other side of the wall, setting down my breakfast tray.

I switch on the light. It's past eight thirty by my little clock. I shake my head, trying to throw off the exhaustion, trying to pull the bare room around me into focus. My fingers are clumsy as I dress myself, my eyes still thick with sleep.

Of course. Sleep. Thick and heavy, the kind I know how to weave.

It seems to take forever before we're left alone, but once the last morning nurse has left I lean over Violeta, excitement crackling in my voice.

"I know how we can get that bracelet away from him. And he'll never even wake up."

I've never actually done this before, but that's true for basically everything I've done since I got to this house. I think of all the deviousness I wasted on things like taking extra-long smoke breaks at work, or accidentally on purpose spilling coffee on the supervisors who couldn't control their wandering hands. Now I'm finally putting it to better use. And, like a good schemer, I do a practice round first.

I remember that you should never cast a sleeping spell without a timing device, unless you want a kind of Sleeping Beauty on your hands, one who'll never be able to wake up, even with a kiss. So on Tuesday night, I make sure to use my hourglass. I've got warm milk and feather pillows; I'm playing the family's well-worn copy of *Moonlight* Sonata, nice and low. I memorize everything I'm doing—the kinds of feathers, the amount of sugar I pour into the milk—so if it works I can do it again, when it's Andrés's turn to sleep.

At eleven o'clock I flip the hourglass over. At 11:09 I put my ear to Mrs. Miramontes's door, hearing nothing but silence.

"Ma'am? I'm sorry to disturb you, but I heard a noise," I call out, softly, in case she's still awake, and when I have no answer I push open the door.

Once again, I feel like I've stepped a hundred years into the past. In the moonlight, everything looks blurry and soft: the gold-and-indigo wallpaper, the velvet-backed chairs, the silver hairbrushes on the dressing table. This room is desperate to return to the days of bustles and horse-drawn carriages, the days when everybody knew their place. Of course, Mrs. Miramontes wouldn't have been able to vote back then, but these people like to ignore stuff like that. I remember now why I wanted to steal anything I could, from this place where they never saw us except to make sure we kept everything polished and shined. I'm itching to steal something again, an impulse I haven't felt in years, but I'm reminded of what else my mother said to me when I stole that handkerchief. "Maybe this was some form of rebellion? But it's you and I who would have borne the cost. Natalia, you've always been more clever than that." And then she looked right at me and said, "And more strategic." Yes, Mom, I am. So I make my hands relax and I remind myself that I'm here to take more from this family than just a handkerchief.

Mrs. Miramontes is wrapped in layers of satin, the bed huge and ornate and cherrywood. She has that soft skin rich women can buy, nourished with Crème de la Mer and Lancôme, no oil burn scars from cooking, not even a hint of sunburn. I want to reach over her face and pull off the mask, revealing the hideous thing underneath.

My watch says 11:10 when I hold my wrist out in the light.

I wave my hand over her sleeping face; no response. None when I rub my hands together, first slowly, then fast. I snap my fingers next to her ear, the sound practically echoing inside me, I'm so coiled and tense. Nothing. I clasp my hand around her wrist and she doesn't stir. I make myself try it again, two more times. Now I have no more excuses.

She's not wearing any necklaces, so I'll have to work with what I've got: her hand, thick with rings. There's a shiny one on her pinky finger, two pearls in an embrace, and I pull it off her, one quarter inch at a time. If I'm caught now I'll be lucky if all they do is throw me in jail.

Her breathing doesn't change as I pull the ring all the way off, and there's a nervous shriek inside my head, begging to escape, as I slide the thing right back into place. She still doesn't stir. Even when I move to her ring finger, and the silver band with the sapphire surrounded by two stones that have to be diamonds. I slide the glittering thing on my own ring finger, and it's a bit loose, but it fits. The moon gleams against the dark blue as I hold up my hand to the light. It's too ornate for me, but it's still the most beautiful thing I've ever had against my skin.

Again the urge to steal wells up inside me. I want so badly to take this, I actually have to close my eyes and recite digits of pi until the urge passes and I can slide it back onto her hand.

My watch ticks on my wrist. It's 11:13. I walk backward out of the room and shut the door slowly, so slowly, and I don't let myself breathe out until it finally clicks.

In the bathroom I throw water on my face over and over, as cold as I can stand it, soaking my thin nightgown. Then I tiptoe to Violeta's bed, her eyes reflecting the glow of the night-light. "I did it, muñeca. She didn't wake up. It can work." And I tell her all of it, the relief spilling out of me in nervous giggles. The joy and triumph are practically radiating from both of us now, shining out from our eyes. I want to pour down a shot of this family's expensive forty-year-old Scotch. I want to reach out and close the distance between me and Violeta, watch her lips tremble as I stroke her black hair.

I want to kiss someone.

I want to kiss her.

My damp face grows hot, and I open the window and let the air cool me down as much as I can before I turn back to her. It's pointless; I know she saw me, flushed and pink.

"Soon. I'll do it soon," I whisper into her ear. "When he comes back from his trip." I can almost see my hands now, pulling that silver bracelet away from his sleeping chest. I'm so full of nervous energy, I'm pacing on the braided rug, and I want to stick my head out the window and shout my triumph into the sky. But there's no shouting in this house.

So when I say good night to Violeta, and shut the door behind myself in my little room, and stroke myself to orgasm, I make sure to cover my mouth with a pillow, so none of my noises escape.

I'm in the kitchen the next morning, pouring my third cup of coffee, when Mrs. Miramontes and Fernanda come in. Mrs. Miramontes is rattling off instructions, something about a ladies' tea on Sunday, tablecloths and furniture polish. She could be a piece of polished furniture herself: her chestnut hair glossy and smooth on her head, her teeth gleaming and white as she greets me, politely, the way one does with the help. But distantly too, the way she often sounds, as though her mind is swirled in layers of fog. I understand now the hazy, blurred woman that Mrs. Miramontes has become. Eyes always a little out of focus, voice a fraction too slow. I don't know what she's taking, but it's enough. Enough to let her pretend she never saw her daughter trying with increasing desperation to call out for help. Mrs. Miramontes always hated anything messy, I remember. Anything scandalous. And what could be more scandalous than a philandering son-in-law and a daughter paralyzed by witchcraft?

I can't let her see those thoughts on my face, so I focus on my coffee, the rich white cream diluting the black, as she prattles on.

"You're so kind, Fernanda, to agree to work a full day on Sunday. We'd be lost without you." *If you really thought that, you'd give her a raise,* my mother would have whispered behind her hand. I glance up at Fernanda, and she catches my eye, just for a flash, and just as quick I decide to drop my placid mask and let her see the expression I'm wearing. It's one I remember from my mother, from Taleitha, from Ruth-Anne. *Aren't they something?* my tight smile and twinkling eyes say to Fernanda, and her eyes seem to say it right back.

"And when did you say Señor Guzmán returns?" Fernanda asks, as if it's an afterthought, but something in her tone sounds like a warning. To me.

"A week from yesterday. Tuesday afternoon." I notice the way Mrs. Miramontes's voice sharpens when she says this, the way it seems to whenever his name comes up.

And then, as if the phone on the wall was listening, it rings, and all three of us jump. Fernanda's face twitches a little as she says hello.

"It's Señor Guzmán," she says, and without a word she hands Mrs. Miramontes the receiver and leaves the room, glancing at me over her shoulder before the door shuts. I hover in the dining room, ear cupped to the heavy doors, where I can only hear a few phrases: ". . . nothing to worry about . . . under control . . . yes, of course." And I can hear my own name, and then again, and her voice higher than it usually is, that genteel detachment gone. Is she giving him a report about me? Andrés strikes me as the kind who could sniff out a plot from two continents away, if he's decided to look for it. When the receiver clicks I rush into the hallway, pretending to pick a few roses from an enormous vase.

"I think Violeta has been left alone long enough, dear, don't you?" Mrs. Miramontes says, and I nod and head up the stairs fast, so she can't see the fear blanching my face.

I don't dare summon Violeta into the doll in the daytime. Not in this house where nobody bothers to knock. So in the mornings I read *Malcolm X* to her, music always on in the background. Violeta chooses the records from the stack I brought from home, or the ones I truck up from the parlor, blinking her *yes* or her *no.* I put up with the Dean Martin she somehow loves, wrinkling my nose theatrically but playing it anyway. I'm much happier when she chooses Nina Simone, that voice that sounds like someone calling, crooning, from another world.

Afternoons are for KBEX, and to my joy they still have *Afternoon Mystery Hour,* which both my mom and my tía Soledad loved to catch whenever they could. The reception struggles a bit to reach us here in the Orinda hills, but we can hear it well enough. The first time they announce the selection, I cackle out loud: It's "Sorry, Wrong Number." A woman stuck in her bed, felled by a mysterious illness, with a husband she regrets having brought into her life.

It's very late Wednesday night, nearly midnight, when I can finally summon Violeta into the doll again. I prop the doll up on my bed, with my door shut. It's not safe but it's the best we can do.

Six years is a long time to go without being able to talk. So I ask her questions and she spells out her answers with the Scrabble tiles I found in the parlor, awkwardly maneuvering the pieces with her stiff hands. I can't imagine this family ever sitting around a table some night, giggling and arguing over what really counted as a word.

"What's your favorite flavor of ice cream?"

Strawberry.

"*Oklahoma* or *West Side Story*?"

My Fair Lady.

"Otis Redding or Aretha Franklin?"

Yes. If her shoulder weren't made of plastic right now, I'd giggle into it, swatting her with a playful fist. "My mother would have agreed with you."

Tell me about her.

The tears leak from my eyes before I can feel them in my chest. Nobody really asks anymore, except Doris. I don't say anything right away; I just leaf through my records, through the slim stack with "Property of Jovita Fuentes" on the front. My hands pause at *Los Grandes Éxitos de Agustín Lara.*

"This was one of her favorite albums. It reminded her of the dance halls she went to when she was young. It's how she met my father. She loved to dance, until she got sick. I can't even remember the last time I played this. . . . I can't stand listening to it alone."

I'm here.

I nod and say nothing and the room fills with the scratch and hiss of the record, the opening notes of "Azul." I feel a tug at my chest, as if someone has threaded the notes in there and just pulled. And the stories come spilling after.

"She worked at the factories during the war, out in Richmond. Eighteen years old, fresh from El Paso, green as a gooseberry, as she liked to say. And on her very first day she makes clear who she is. The ladies always sat at segregated lunch tables, see. Nobody told them to; they just did. And she grabbed her lunch pail and she sat herself down at a whole table full of Black women, and when the other Mexicans were shooting daggers at her she just smiled at the ladies at her table and started passing around her sister's homemade tortillas. Within six months she was trying to organize a union. I wish you'd known that side of her. Fearless."

I wish I had too.

"When she was dying"—my chest tightens as I speak that phrase out loud, but when I'm done it feels like I've shoved aside some heavy thing I've been carrying next to my ribs all these years—"she was more angry than afraid. She had so much she still wanted to do. She said it all the time, how the best thing any of us can do is find what our talent is, and use it to do some good. And instead she ended up . . ."

Working here, Violeta finishes for me.

"Yeah. Working here. Instead of being a union organizer or maybe a teacher. She was going to try again when I was grown and out of school. And then instead she watched me get my diploma and then two months later she got diagnosed with cancer and then she died. Happened to a bunch of her friends from the factories. Got them all in the lungs. It's the kind of injustice that she might have spent her life fighting against. If it hadn't, you know, killed her first.

"But you know what she never did, even when she knew it was the end? She never told me stuff like, 'You have to do this or that with your life, m'ija, because of what I went through, all the sacrifices I made for you.' That's a weight she didn't want me to carry—her hopes. She only wanted me to carry my own."

The little dolly face looks up at me for a long time before she spells out her response.

You must miss her so much.

This hits me so hard, I collapse onto the bed. I can let the sobs go this time, knowing Andrés isn't on the other side of that wall and can't hear. I've cried plenty for my mother, but somehow these tears feel . . . different. Like they're filling a crevice I thought I could never reach. Forming a pool, still and quiet.

When I return Violeta to her body, her eyes flutter open, and they don't leave me while I press my hand into hers, while I count what remains until Andrés is back, with that key shining around his perfumed neck. Five days. Agustín Lara sings to us both, about the blue color of dawn.

By the next night I'm done with sad songs, and I set the cookie tin by Violeta's bed, my voice thrumming with mischief.

"You want to see something fun?" I ask her.

Yes, her doll head nods.

"You're not afraid of bugs, are you?"

No.

So I open the tin and pull out an envelope full of pieces of paper, tiny bits like confetti. Cut from sheet music, then cured in rum inside old ballet shoes. I throw open the window, letting in the warm air, and then I pull down the shade and turn off every light except the one by her bedside. Soon, moths find their way to the window, drawn by the gleam in the dark.

Now I pull up the shade and a flight of moths flutters in, and I cup the paper bits in my hands and sprinkle them over the beating wings. Then I start up the record player on low, and as the music swells, the moths form a single long line through the air, like migrating birds. Or like shadow puppets, with little brown wings. And now that line dips and sways to the tune, forming long, lazy arcs through the stale air of her room. Violeta's plastic face turns and turns, following their flight over our heads, her doll arms open wide, as Nina sings the opening lines of one of my favorite songs: "I Put a Spell on You."

When the song ends, they drop their formation, and if moths could look bewildered, these would. I open the window and shoo them away and turn to Violeta, her pale doll's arms still reaching for the sky.

There, again, is the rush of that power, shot through with joy. I wonder if my grandmother ever used her spells to do any good. Pretty sure she never bothered to ask herself questions like that. I wonder if she's ever felt the way I do now, like the music and the wonder are both singing through my arms and my hands, ready to soak through the walls.

~

On Friday evening Mrs. Miramontes sails into the room in a midnight-blue organza dress, on her way to some charity ball. She's sliding a lotion onto her hands, a scent I know from some of the bankers' wives when they visit our offices: heavy florals, like a rose kept a day or two past its prime. Hypnotique, one of them told me when I asked what her perfume was called, her tone saying she was conveying a great favor by speaking to me.

"You're working miracles with my daughter," Mrs. Miramontes says in that distant way of hers, lifting up Violeta's chin, pulling up her nightgown, feeling for the first signs of bedsores. She reminds me of a shopper checking a peach for sugar spots.

"Her color is so much better, and she's no longer just sleeping all day."

That's because I know she's a person with a mind, and not a lump in a La Perla nightgown, I don't say to her. I just nod and thank her and remember what it felt like to wear her ring on my hand.

"What a beautiful dress, Mrs. Miramontes. May I?" I ask, stroking the gown's bustling skirts. When she rustles away in a rose-scented trail, I take the loose blue thread I pulled from her gown and tuck it into the cookie tin. I watch Violeta's eyes follow her on the way out the door, and I can see the fury in them now, the screaming wish to be free. An idea tugs at me, following me even as I head to the kitchen. Like a teenager begging to be allowed to go to a dance.

I remember Violeta once, when she was fifteen or sixteen, doing something very like that. Some distant aunt and uncle and their teenage kids were visiting for the holiday, and I was in the parlor, putting their records and their games away. Violeta was in the next room—or in the hallway? Memories are slippery sometimes—and she was chattering excitedly to her mother, something about an extra concert ticket her cousins had. It was Screamin' Jay Hawkins at Sweet's Ballroom, a place Taleitha's kids liked to go. I heard the phrases "public school kids" and "bad influence" and "no daughter of mine." Later that day I was helping my mother empty the wastebaskets and I saw it, tossed in Violeta's trash: a sheet of paper with a little figure, crudely drawn, a pile of chestnut-colored hair on her head, her paper ears pocked with holes the size of a pin. I reached for the paper and my mother shook her head and she made sure it went straight into the outside bin.

~

"You were trying to make a voodoo doll?" I ask Violeta after I remind her of this story.

Yes.

One of the women at the bank, Céline, grew up in Haiti, and she had a lot to say about white people trying to pick up her religion like it was the latest hairstyle. But, like a whole lot of things I'm aching to talk about with Violeta, this isn't the time. Not yet. I still have to admire the spirit, that streak of darkness curled inside that small frame. A darkness that saw its own twin, maybe, when I came here with my box of spells. I take a long breath and then pick up the bowl of strawberries I brought back from the kitchen and I run my fingers along the reddest of the berries, my fingers stroking the seeds.

"I always feel guilty when I eat in front of you," I tell her, pointing to the feeding tube that hides in wait under her gown. "Especially these. My mom told me you once ate three helpings of strawberries and cream, when you thought nobody saw." There's that elusive blush again, her cheeks stained red.

"But she would say, 'Guilt is like fear. It's there to help guide your attention to something. Not for carrying around like a millstone.'"

So I take the berry in my hand and bite into it, just enough to release the juice, and I dip my finger into the red. And I lean over and ask Violeta for permission for what I'm about to do and only then do I gently, so gently, open her lips, my eyes fixed on hers, ready to stop the second she blinks her *no.* Then I slide my red-painted finger over her tongue, and I can see it in her eyes the instant she can taste the juice, maybe the first time she's tasted anything in six years. And when I swallow the rest of the berry, it feels like I've pulled it straight from the vine, ripe and quivering.

"I've got an idea, muñeca. But it comes with some rules." And I spell each one out, and with each one her eyes blink their *yes.* We both watch the clock as it sweeps on toward midnight, when the house will be asleep and it will be safe. Safe enough.

TWELVE

At midnight I creep through the door, on the pretense of filling my water jug, so I can feel the quiet all over the house. When I get back to Violeta's room, my entire body is trembling, and I keep dropping my materials, even the spell card, on the floor. My hands shake, remembering that sting as my grandmother slapped her card out of my hand. That warning, the warning I'm ignoring now.

I hold up the hourglass, and I tell Violeta that she has to be back to make the switch before the last grain of sand drops through.

"Otherwise I might be stuck in your body forever," I warn her, pulling the Nina Simone album from its case and settling the needle into its groove. "Understood?"

Yes.

"I trust you," I say, to myself as much as to her, not bothering to still the shaking in my voice.

Now I take the braided lock of Violeta's hair that I cut off yesterday, and this time instead of weaving it into the little doll's blond hair, I weave it into a lock of my own, her slippery black and my earthy brown. The music is so rich in this silent place that I can practically feel it, as if I could pull the song from the air and wrap it around the both of us.

"Are you sure this is all right?"

Yes.

"Can I kiss you?"

Yes. But as the thrill begins to soak through me I have to know something else.

"Do you want me to kiss you?"

Yes. Yes.

Yes.

I can see her heartbeat thrumming through her nightgown, and I want so much to touch that heartbeat, to feel the swell of her breast, before I lean in for a kiss.

"Can I touch you?"

Yes.

But I only trace my fingers along her lips, feeling her breath catch once, twice, again, and when she finally lets it out it's as though every breath she's held in for six years comes sighing out all at once and my own breath shudders out of my body and I want more. Her thin nightgown is still too thick, too completely in the way, and I want to reach under the covers and pull it aside, watch her eyes widen as my nails graze her waist.

But I don't. She's trapped inside that body, and it's time to let her out. Her mouth is open, slack and panting in a way I love seeing on a woman, knowing what I can do next, but I lean over now and I lick her top lip, then the bottom lip, and I feel like my beating heart is trying to escape into my mouth as I press my lips against hers. I feel so warm and so very soft, and it's like the night when Doris took me to that party, when Carla Thomas's voice soared so high and free, and when I walked out the thin door of that apartment looking just the same, but very different from when I walked in.

THIRTEEN

My love,

Will that word frighten you? I don't know, but I know how much my hands have itched to write it. And I don't intend to throw away this chance.

I've never been in love before. Have you? I like to imagine you have, with some lucky woman. I honestly never thought of loving a woman as something I could do. I remember the dances back at school, all of us giggling and trying to teach each other the mambo. How much I looked forward to dancing with my friends Frances and Elsie, how deflated I always felt when the night would end. I might have loved one of them, maybe, if I'd let myself imagine it. If I'd thought of it as something I was allowed to do.

But no more dipping into the past. This night will end for me too, and you will be back in your body, and I want to tell you everything. I have twenty-one minutes left by the watch on my wrist. Your wrist, that I am only borrowing.

So: It started when my lips were on yours and yours were on mine and the joy was so complete that I thought that was the magic, right there. Me melting into you, you into me. And then I opened my eyes and I stood up and my hands were your hands. I ran my hands over my arms, and felt my warm skin, and it was your skin, but just then, it was mine. It felt so wonderful to make my hands move, to dance in the air, like shadow puppets. I turned to the mirror and there I was. Inside your body, looking out from your eyes. And behind me in the mirror I could see my body, and inside it was you, Nati.

I called your name, but no response; no sign, except your breath, that you were in there at all. I did panic, for a second. I nearly kissed you, to switch us back. But I just had to taste that freedom, and trust that it would all work as you said it would. That we'd be back in our bodies as long as I got back before the sand slipped through.

I won't lie to you. I stood with my hand on the door to my mother's room and wanted so badly to open it. I wanted to stand over her, shouting her awake, with one of her crystal vases in my hand. But it would be your hand holding that crystal, not mine, and it's your body that would be handcuffed and sent off to jail. So I used all my strength to back away from that door. It's very good, for both of us, that Andrés isn't back from his trip. I won't write here what I want to happen to him. It would burn the page.

The thing is, I didn't really want to use that vase. What I wanted was to be inside my own body again. And for her to be stuck inside hers. I wanted to stand over her frozen face and ask her, "Why? Why? What could you possibly have got out of letting me rot all these years?" And her not able to answer, of course, which is just as well. Because what answer would be good enough?

And yes, I thought of escape. Rifling through the drawers for silver, maybe even cash if I knew where to find some, taking off into the night. I got as far as the coat hook by the door, where the car keys hang. And then I saw my face in the hallway mirror. Your face, that I was borrowing, while you were stuck inside my own body, upstairs. And the only one who could free you from it is . . . you.

I knew exactly what Andrés or my mother would do. And I also knew I didn't want anything to do with those people ever again. Not with them, or with the way they look at the world, as if everything and everyone in it was put there for them to use.

So I left the keys and I crept along the hallway, with this diary in my apron, writing lines and touching everything as I went. In the kitchen, I stood staring at the refrigerator, clean and bright and full of food I could pick up for myself, and taste, and eat. Before I even touched the handle my mouth was already watering. I was ready to devour everything I might find.

And there it was. A little plate on the middle shelf, with a note: "Nati's midnight snack." What a sly game you were playing, hoping I would come down and see it, but knowing that anyone else also might. Crackers, chocolate, olives, a wedge of Gruyère. A jar of amber liquid that, when I opened it, was a few inches of sweet Jerez. Enough for me to feel a little softer, a little warmer; not enough for a hangover that you'd feel when you woke. And strawberries, with a dish of whipped cream you must have made for me. Every part of me grew open and eager, thinking of you laying those things on that plate. My mouth watered so much that if anyone had seen it they would think me grotesque.

But you wouldn't.

The chill air seemed to wake up my skin as I pulled the berries from their stems and swirled the juice between my lips, as I felt the crumbly salt of the cheese on my tongue. The richness was like a wave crashing through my body, starting at my mouth.

I closed the fridge door and took the plate out to the garden. (Please don't rush there to clean up; I tidied the kitchen as though somebody were watching me. And I was very careful with the squeaky door.)

The night was warm, one of those nights when the moonlight feels like a bath. I touched everything: the brick of the flagstones, rough on my palms. The roses, pink and soft; even the scratch of the thorns felt good, because it was a sensation I chose. There were the gardenias, the kind you bring into my room. I plucked one of them from its stem, warm in my hands, and slipped it inside the cup of your bra, for you to find when you're back in your body.

I felt my silence like a drum inside my chest, and I wanted so badly to shout something, anything, just to make a sound exist in the world. But there was no way for me to do this without it coming back to hurt you. And then I realized what I could do.

I spent those last few minutes of freedom with the taste of chocolate and strawberries still in my mouth, singing, just under my breath, too softly for anyone to hear but me. "I Put a Spell on You," of course. And one you played for me just today, my voice nearly cracking at the words: "I Shall Be Released."

FOURTEEN

In the morning I wake with pain in my skull that throbs whenever I move, and Violeta's letter over my face, the letter that opens with the words "My love."

I fell in love when I was twenty-one, right after I moved into Doris's place. Her name was Olivia. She showed up at one of the house parties Doris and I went to, graceful as a cat in her tangerine dress, her eyes made up with thick kohl. I found my way to her side with a drink, and I stayed there even as everyone else shuffled and reshuffled around us. She started visiting me, but she could never stay the night; she still lived at home. After we made love I would lie in the space she left in the bed and smell the pillowcases that still held her scent. I went to dinner at her house a few times, disguised as merely a friend, and I'd have to sit across from her at the table acting like everything was normal, politely passing along a serving dish. I had no idea how everyone didn't smell it on me, on us, that feeling even sweeter than lust, somehow earthier and more heavenly.

It's what's happening to me this morning, as the family's doctor comes by to do his monthly checkup; as Fernanda vacuums and dusts. I have no memory of the time I spent inside

Violeta's body last night; it was like a long sleep, dreamless and quiet. I should probably wonder why that is, and maybe think about where this pain in my head is coming from, why it's not responding to the aspirin I've gulped down. But all of that fades to the background when I remember that kiss.

I can't let myself look at Violeta when anyone's around, so I concentrate on changing the records, sliding each into its white sleeve, and on my reading (something tells me to stick to *Rebecca* when the doctor is here). When nobody's looking I catch Violeta's eye, just for an instant, and then I tap my apron pocket, where she can see the outline of the letter she left me last night, the slight weight of it brushing my thigh.

My head is still pounding when I go downstairs, and I can't shake the thought that somehow this is a lingering toll, a side effect of that spell. It doesn't help that the midmorning sky is cloudy and damp, the air clinging to me when I step outside. All the same, it's strange to see Rosario in the parlor fussing over the fireplace, her face growing even more wrinkles. "Why a fire in May?" I ask her, that sense of mischief tingling in me again.

"Making sure the chimney is all clear and everything works. Mrs. Miramontes said the ladies might want to do a séance tomorrow." Rosario crosses herself.

"Wouldn't a dinner party be a better time for that kind of thing?"

"Those are more expensive."

She's more talkative than Fernanda, that's for sure. I kneel beside her and start handing her the pieces of firewood. "So does Miss Violeta have a lot of different nurses?"

"Different nurses, different everybody. Nobody stays long here."

"Why is that?" I keep my voice as soft as the fire consuming the newsprint.

"I'm not sure. But nobody does, especially the ones who take care of her. I hope I can stay long. I need this job."

The logs begin to catch, and the smoke sweeps up through the chimney, just as it should. I help Rosario sweep the hearth clean and pull the grate closed, and then she goes to answer the service bell. Before she can come back, I take out the letter, the one I promised Violeta I would burn, and I read my favorite part (*even the scratch of the thorns felt good, because it was a sensation I chose*).

I feed the paper to the flames, and the black heat licks at the edges before consuming the whole trembling thing.

I head back upstairs to Violeta when Dr. Levin's finally gone, lingering at the coat hook where the keys are, the keys Violeta did not take. I know what Doris would say: that it's possible Violeta is just playing a long game. Confessing to a half-baked plan that she conveniently dropped, so I'll trust her a bit more the next time. Like unspooling a length of rope, foot by foot, until it's long enough for a real escape.

But there's a flower next to my heart, one that Violeta picked for me, in her one precious hour of freedom. Where she passed a test she had no idea she'd been given.

"I lied to you. Last night." I hold up the hourglass, the sand swaying back and forth. "I didn't use this in the spell last night. There was no time limit. I just told you there was."

I let this sink in, and then I ask, "Do you understand why I lied?"

Yes.

"I'm sorry. I had to know I could trust you to come back. And you did." She doesn't look away, doesn't blush. Yes, I am unspooling more rope. I can practically feel it now, hissing through my hands, the roughness, the heat. I tuck away a lock of her hair again, behind her ear.

"So . . . tonight is Saturday night. Would you like to go somewhere? Where you can dance?"

The only phones in the house that the help are allowed to use are in the kitchen and the parlor, with no privacy as long as anyone is around. So I have to wait until late afternoon, when Mrs. Miramontes is shopping, and Fernanda and Rosario have gone home for the day. Then only the walls can hear me dial my home number, pacing as the phone rings and rings, before someone finally picks up and Doris's voice crackles through on the line.

"Natalia Fuentes. As I live and breathe." Her mom's Mississippi accent comes through when she's annoyed or upset. "The one who promised to call and update us now and then." When I don't respond she continues: "I mean, there's so much to catch up on." And then guilt twists my stomach as I remember what I haven't thought of once all week, the conversation Doris and I spent a whole afternoon preparing her for, taking a page out of Mom's union-organizing playbooks, role-playing and practicing until Doris had it down.

"Doris! Did you talk to your boss? Did you get your promotion?" And then Doris's laughter pours right through the old-fashioned receiver, into the parlor's still air.

"I sure did. You're talking to the new senior floor supervisor. When he balked, I told him he could sign either my new promotion papers or my two weeks' notice." My mother and Doris never met, but there's that same thread running through them both. More like a rope, woven tight and strong.

"I'm so happy for you. You should be running that place."

"I know I should. Oh, and we're having a party next week, to celebrate. Just a little one." I can hear in Doris's voice exactly what kind of party she means. Like the one she took me to, like the ones where we've met half of our lovers and our friends.

"Wait, what happened to not wanting the landlord to figure out who he's renting to? Or did he die and this is your way of telling me?" I wish I could bottle her laughter as it pours through the phone line. It's more joy than I've heard all week.

"No. I just decided I'm tired of being afraid of him. I have to put on a mask every time I walk out that door. I've accepted that, but I'll be damned if I'll wear one inside my own home." Now I hear a woman's voice on the other end of the line, unfamiliar and musical, and the sound of a giggling kiss.

"Is that your latest girl?" I can practically hear Doris blushing. At the bank, she always has to appear impeccable, unflappable, strict. It helps the white supervisors feel safe. It's always fun to hear her going giggly and soft like this.

"Yessssss. Her name's Andrea. She's a friend of Lupe's and she's coming dancing with us tonight. What time am I picking you up?"

"So . . . about that." As I talk I can hear her suck in her breath, and I know it's impossible, but it feels like she doesn't let that breath out the whole time I tell her everything that's happened this week, and why I'm asking her to take my body out dancing . . . but with someone else in it.

"Waaaaaaait a minute." Doris's heels click over the floor, and when she speaks again it sounds like she must have brought the phone into her room. "Only two weeks ago you were my cautious little friend who was the fastest calculator on three floors and liked to point out the tricks at the magic shows. Now you're talking sleeping spells and how you let some girl . . . possess your body, and each thing you're telling me is scarier than the last. And I know you're not lying, and I don't think you're delusional, which means at least some of it has to be true."

Another breath, this time raggedy and long.

"So listen, Nati . . . I'm not actually asking you to tell me why you're doing all this, because this is your life and you get to figure this out. But *you* at least know why. Right?"

My reasons have been slippery and elusive, even for me, since I came to this house, shifting every time I examine them. But now, hearing my friend's voice sounding like home, my reasons emerge, clear and bright.

So many are about Violeta. The trust in her face that I will rescue her, that I won't walk away and leave her here. The memory of her facing off against her mother without seeming to, defending me without saying a word. Her hunger for life, despite being trapped for so long. The way she's unafraid of the streaks of darkness in her soul. A darkness that was always there, hidden, maybe even from Violeta herself, that's been swelling inside her for six years, bitter and strong. Her embrace of it, spelling it out, plain and clear: *Kill them.* And of course, that kiss, the words she wrote me, using my own pen, my own hands.

But I think the reason is actually me, and who I've become since walking through the heavy door of this house. No more of that quiet, reserved girl at the corner desk, wearing my everyday face. No more dulling my brain with percentages, busying my hands with stacks of checks and deposit slips. I'm inventing spells all on my own now, my hands wielding a power that comes when I call it. No more of that plain brown wrapping for me. Just the thought of wearing that costume again makes my skin itch. I'm so grateful that Doris isn't actually asking me to tell her any of this, because I couldn't hide it from her and I couldn't lie.

"I know why. And I'll tell you someday."

"I hope you also know that you've fallen in love with this girl," Doris says. "Pretty fast, too."

I miss my friend so much my chest hurts. "If you don't want to do this, I'll understand, really. You should only do it if you're sure."

There's nothing on the line but a very long sigh.

"I'll do it. And you're sure that you trust her?"

As soon as I say the word *yes* out loud, I know it's true.

"This girl's white, isn't she?"

"Might as well be, yes."

Another silence, this one longer than the first. "All right. But you owe me, you know that? I'll be there at seven. Tell her to remember that she's a guest, several times over. And I have no problem sending a guest back to her fancy house if she doesn't know how to act."

FIFTEEN

My love,

I am leaving this for you, for when you are back in your body, so you can read all about my sweet night of freedom, thanks to you. And so you will know what it felt like to be inside your body, making love to you.

Do I tease you? Good. I'm going to tell this in order, as well as I can. It didn't start with lovemaking; it never does.

It started again with your mouth on mine, and if there is anything more delicious—even those berries, even that Jerez—I've never tasted it. I stood up and there I was, in your going-out dress, a little peach-colored thing that showed off your legs. My legs, for the night. I took one last look at my body in the bed, with you shut up inside it, before I walked down the stairs. As I passed the parlor I could smell my mother's perfume, and hear the click of her solitaire cards.

When she called out, "Have a pleasant evening, dear," I did not run into the room and strangle her with the curtains. I did not spill her hot tea all over her face. I just thanked her and fairly ran for the door, where Doris's car was already pulling up.

"I'm Violeta," I said, from inside your body. She looked me up and down.

"Oh, I know."

If I had days to write this, I'd tell you everything in full detail, scene by scene. Instead I'll tell you pieces: the breeze on my face as we drove with all the windows open, the lights of the city as we drove toward downtown. Doris letting me babble away about nothing until it was time to pick up her date, Andrea, who Doris warned me knew nothing of our secret, who just thought I was you. She parked and we walked along Telegraph Avenue, three women in bright dresses and fresh lipstick. We kept passing groups of men, and some of them whistled and leered. One of them even reached out his hand to grab at my waist, and I flinched. Doris took a look at my face.

"Treat you differently in this body, don't they?" she murmured when Andrea couldn't hear. I wasn't sure how to respond, so I didn't. After a second she reached into her purse and pulled out something that her wide grin told me was not a hand-rolled cigarette. Boarding-school Violeta would never have touched the stuff, but boarding-school Violeta hadn't spent six years staring at yellow flowers on the walls. It took me maybe half a

dozen sputtering tries, but I finally drew some of the smoke into my lungs. And if I felt wonderful and flying before, now I was a twinkling star, watching my giggling self open the door of Sweet's Ballroom, a place I wanted to go as a teenager and never could. A place where the entire room might as well have been made of doors, all of them opening, all at once. There were dresses in every rainbow color, and the band was playing something fast with trumpet and saxophone, and when I touched the speaker the music thumped under my hand.

We'd barely sat down when a smiling man approached Andrea right away, and she winked at Doris and me before he pulled her onto the dance floor. Doris sat with me for a song, while I tried to work up the courage to dance. I haven't said how radiant she looked. She glowed in a purple dress, cut to her thighs, and shoes I would die for. Bright turquoise wedge heels. Out of nowhere, she leaned over to me, talking loud enough for me to hear her over the crowd.

"My family hasn't talked to me for eleven years. Since I refused to renounce my 'lifestyle.'"

"I'm sorry."

"Don't be. It's their loss." She meant it, I could tell. How I admired her then, Nati. Almost as much as I admire you.

"I'm telling you this so you know that Nati isn't just any old friend. And if you hurt her, if you think she's just a ticket to go back to your rich family, your rich life—"

"I have no family, Doris," I said. And I told her what I haven't yet told you, although it won't surprise you one bit.

"Six years ago I learned that my husband liked to step out with other women. He wasn't even subtle about it. I didn't love him, but I still wouldn't stand for being humiliated. But when I went to my mother, she told me that women in our family were expected to swallow their pride. That men couldn't control their urges. And that we needed Andrés's money. So never mind my self-respect, or my pride. I couldn't believe it. It was like she'd been wearing some mask her whole life and she had just taken it off. Worse, she was trying to pass it on to me, for me to wear."

Doris sat very still as I told her all this, and in her eyes I saw a little glimmer of understanding.

"Nati is the only person in that house who cares what I want," I told her. "Or who's even tried to find out what that is."

You are so fortunate, my love, to have her as your friend. Because she held my gaze, and then she said: "I believe you. And all the same, if you do her wrong, I'll find you, and I'll forget about all those hippie peace petitions I ever signed. Understand?"

And I nodded, and then two young men in shiny suits were standing over us, asking us both to dance. It took two songs, three songs, for me to learn to dance in the new shape of your body, but my dancing partner—Daniel? David?—was so patient and kind, and before long I had it down. I could feel the thump of the bass against the floor, the sweat beading on my skin, and every time he asked if I wanted to stop I said I wanted to keep going, as long as I could. Doris checked on me every so often, and then sailed back away with her partner. I could see her and Andrea sometimes glance at each other over their dance partners' shoulders, and I knew just how they felt.

David—Daniel?—was a beautiful young man, the kind I used to imagine would be my ideal mate. Don't worry, Nati. I felt nothing at all for him, even with his kind smile and his consideration, bringing me water when I got too flushed. Instead I was aching, so badly, to be dancing with you.

Yes, I did look at that exit sign, the side door that opened to Broadway. On my way back from the ladies' room I imagined slipping through it in that thin dress, barely ten dollars in my purse. And where could I go? I could walk to a police station. Tell the officers that I wasn't really a Mexican American housemaid, but that I was actually the last living heiress of the Spanish general Mariano Vásquez Del Valle, and I was just borrowing the housemaid's body for a night. And that I was imploring them to help me rescue the bewitched heiress from her mansion in the Orinda hills. I only wondered how quickly they'd send for the van and the men in white coats.

You're the most clever person I've ever known, Nati. It's one of the things I admire about you. So you know there's a chance that, even now, I'm just telling you what you want to hear. But I think you know how much I hate the idea of that pair of ghouls, as you call them, getting away with everything. I wanted to make them both pay. And I thought that if I waited, if I trusted you, maybe I could. So I dried my hands and let my dancing partner pull me back out on the floor, feeling the thrill of the drums under my feet.

At the end of the night Doris came to rescue me before he could offer me his phone number or ask to see me again. We stumbled down the sidewalk, giggling, and I was reminded of those dances at school, my friends Frances and Elsie, laughing and spinning me around. That moment, right there, was the sweetest of the whole night. So far, anyway.

When Doris pulled up in the driveway again, every window was dark, like the house was asleep. I thanked her for the evening, twice, putting off the moment I would have to get out of the car and head back through that door.

"You're welcome. I'm glad you got to get out, just for a little. I hope one day it can be for real. Truly. And until then, you remember what I said." And then she walked around the car, like a gentleman, and opened the door, and I had to go inside the house, and it felt like I was crawling back inside the jaws of a beast.

But there was something else too, because I knew what I was going to do with my body—your body—the second I could. And if it wasn't well after midnight, I would have run up those stairs.

In my room I stood watching my own body in my own bed, holding you somewhere inside. And then I took off your peach-colored dress and stood in front of the mirror and I looked at my figure. At your figure. Those muscles and bones that had let me dance, and whirl, and laugh. It took my breath away, it was so beautiful. The shine of sweat from my dancing, the face I had wanted so many times to touch. I ran a hand over my—your—soft freckled cheeks, down your neck.

Then I left my own sleeping body behind and quietly, very quietly, cracked open the door to your little room, empty and holding no traces of you. As if your body lived there, but nothing of your soul. The sheets were coarse and stiff as I slid under them, the blanket scratchy and smelling of mothballs, but they felt richer to me in that moment than the Waldorf Astoria. Forgive my extravagance, but it's true.

I slid my hands along my waist—your waist, that I can never pay you back for letting me borrow—and it was hot against my hands and I nestled my nose against my inner wrist, smelling dear and familiar. It was the lavender soap the nurses always use for my sponge baths, the soap you bathed your own body with this evening, before getting dressed up. It was your way of signaling to me now, right now, that you thought of me as the shower flowed over you. I loved it and I felt wetter between my thighs. I wanted to open them and feel it for myself, and I began narrating in my head this letter to you. It's how I can tell you just how soft my nipple felt under my hands, until I clasped it and the skin hardened and, fascinated, I did it again to the other one, and my breath came out in little gasps. So this is what it meant. This is what it could be like.

I ran my hand down my stomach and along my thighs, and I felt how smooth your skin was, how warm, how my legs parted for my hands, before I could even think to command them. This was so different from young Violeta, cowering under the covers, fumbling at myself, wondering why I didn't feel anything at the thought of Andrés, or the two boys I dated briefly before him, in those two dead years after boarding school. Frigid, I thought I was then. Cold.

And then I thought of my own body on the other side of the wall, with you trapped inside it, frozen and still, and it was like ice water down my spine. I sat up and shook the thought loose from my head, and began to write more of these lines. And the deep black ink moved across the page, under a hand I could control, a hand that was mine until dawn. I thought of you tomorrow, back in your body—this body—and of the flush that's going to stain your cheeks and your neck while you read. And then I grew wet again, and open, and slick. So I put down the pen and the book.

Don't worry, my love: I won't tease you without satisfaction. Here's what I did after I put those things down. I slid my fingers into my mouth—your mouth, and it is so much lusher than mine—and I tasted myself. Tasted you. I'd never known anything so sweet, so soft. I pictured you, in your bed, touching yourself, reading these words. I wondered what it would be like to be back in my own body someday, free and feeling every bit of your weight on mine. I started to feel myself, coiled and still for six years, like a rope of silk, loosening. I filled my mouth with your thin pillow as my orgasm came, so it was only the flowered pillowcase that heard me whispering your name, again and again and again.

SIXTEEN

The last time I did this spell the punishment was a cloud of pain, swirling inside my head. This time, it's more like a slow vise, gripping my temples as I move. It tightens with the noise of the house waking up around me: the service bell announcing the men delivering cakes and flowers, the windows opening to the fresh air. I gulp down four aspirin, just like yesterday, but just like yesterday they do nothing, and now the nurse is here, checking Violeta's feeding tube, checking her vital signs. She's a different nurse than before, of course. *Nobody stays long here.*

I shouldn't dare summon Violeta into the doll, not during the day. But I can't wait until tonight to communicate. Not anymore. I've done so many risky things since coming here, and this is just another step I'm taking into madness. Nobody's going to bother with us this morning anyway; downstairs they're too busy using flower arrangements to cover cracks in the wallpaper, sliding chairs over threadbare patches of carpet and tablecloths over water spots on the wood.

"Today's your mother's luncheon," I tell Violeta, setting her blond pigtails against my thin pillow, her glass eyes swiveling up to my face. "They're getting everything ready. Sandwiches and sherry and tea. Maybe she'll take them on a little tour of the house: Here are the portraits of my Spanish ancestors, with the land stolen from the Indians; here is the silver tea set, brought about from their suffering and their blood; here is my daughter, who I let languish here because standing up to my rich son-in-law would be too messy, and I'd have to sell more land, maybe my silver tea set."

These thoughts make a little smirk creep up the corner of my mouth. "Imagine if that tea set could talk." *There's misery in every beautiful thing in this house*, my mother said to me that evening, thin streaks of black on her white polishing cloth. "Imagine the suffering it could tell of, all those Indians toiling in the silver mines."

I know this might make Violeta uncomfortable; she probably never thought about any of this before, let alone when she drank from it. But I'm my mother's daughter, and I don't care. And the pale hand moves the tiles, spelling out, *I wish it could.*

And now an idea can't help but bloom inside me, rich and delicious. What if I could make that happen? Exactly that?

Rosemary and sage are good for my purposes—in my hands they can dredge up anyone's memories—and so I steal to the garden and snip a handful of sprigs with the family's garden shears. I love the way the shears feel in my hand, so heavy and sharp. The herbs get locked inside a jewelry box, so I can unlock them again, and only then do I crush them and stir them into a jar of salve, unscented and clear. The vise keeps its hold on my skull.

Violeta told me her mother used to sing "Amazing Grace" to her when she was little, a lullaby to send a fussy Violeta to sleep. Probably just whenever their nursemaid was sick. But it will dredge up memories, so it'll do just fine, especially when I find a recording of that song in the parlor. It's by Mahalia Jackson, and she used to sing this for the civil rights marchers, so I don't know how it got to this dusty place. Then I see it, stamped on the inside flap: "From the collection of Taleitha Phillips," and again I stifle a laugh. It's almost like Taleitha getting in a little stab of revenge after Mrs. Miramontes fired her—after she'd served this family more than thirty years.

In Violeta's room, she's back inside her body, her black eyes watching me smear the herbed salve over the teapot, and on the silver rim of one of the cups. Just one. "Sing your songs of pain," I tell the tea set, while Mahalia Jackson sings to us both, in that low, velvety contralto that I wish I could let fill up the room. "Of the ones who mined this metal. Let your stories be heard, after so many years."

I should not be doing this. I should be worrying about the ache in my skull, and why it's still here. But Mrs. Miramontes is so good at turning away from suffering; the idea of giving her a taste of it is too tempting.

Don't fool yourself, little girl, my grandmother would say. *You're doing this because you want to. And because you can.*

Five minutes later, the polished pot is ready for Fernanda to fill with hot water, the tea loose and waiting, and there's a very special teacup in Mrs. Miramontes's usual place. Rosemary sprigs are in the flower arrangements, to cover the smell of the salve. Excitement and fear are both running through me, like a thread of electrical current, thrumming and hot.

The sounds of *Afternoon Mystery Hour* trail down the stairs from Violeta's room, a little louder than usual. We're listening to the program together, everyone will think. Just like we have every afternoon. I duck into the library, right next to the parlor, as the doorbell rings. The first of the ladies are here.

Mom tried to keep me away from the Miramontes house as much as she could. But four or five times a year, I'd come help out, usually for their big parties, the ones that shrank as their fortune did. Mom never let me serve the guests; I had to stay in the kitchen, chopping the vegetables or scrubbing the pots.

"But it's hot and full of old ladies," I remember whining to her.

"Exactly. It's the gentlemen you have to watch out for."

When she could steal a moment, though, we'd sneak into the library, which they never opened up for the guests. There was an old speaking tube in the wall, from the house's Victorian phase; the brass speaking bell and long wires were long gone, but the round tube served perfectly as a tiny peephole into the parlor. We'd sneak looks at the beautiful party dresses, the food we'd spent hours sculpting and setting on plates. Mom would make up nicknames for everyone ("Snobby Von Clutchypearls," "Slurpy McDrinksalot") and we'd fight to keep our giggles in check.

The speaking tube is still there, and it's my turn to give these ladies their names. There's Besos, because she insists on kissing everyone on the cheek; Clicky Heels, with a quiet mouth and very loud platform shoes; and the one I'm calling Kitty, because she sounds like she's watched Eartha Kitt as Catwoman a few too many times.

Their talk swirls around the room like the smoke from Kitty's long, narrow cigarettes, dipping in and out of earshot: ". . . it's the best spy novel I've ever read . . ." (that's Besos); "Well, what did they expect . . . running wild on those campuses . . ." (Clicky Heels); "I mean, of course . . . couldn't admit her; she's a *divorcée* . . ." (That's Kitty, and at the word *divorcée* I can see Mrs. Miramontes's reaction, looking like someone reached out from behind her and tightened the strings of her face.)

I can hear them better as they settle at the mahogany table near the library door, covered in lace doilies, the silver pot gleaming in the middle. Mrs. Miramontes reaches for the tea, and I can smell the scent of jasmine and bergamot. I sing, soft as a breath, "How precious did that grace appear / The hour I first believed . . ." Her hands are steady and smooth as she picks up the teapot, but I can see when they begin to shake. She glances around the table, finding nothing but three curious faces, four empty cups on saucers waiting for her to fill them. The way generations of Miramontes women have done before her, the line that for generations stayed European and pure as the silver itself.

Liquid splashes into the cups, and my chest grows warmer with every pour, as I watch her shaking hands spill tea on the saucers, on the doilies below. The ladies pretend not to notice, instead making polite little *mmmm* sounds at the cute little tea sandwiches, crusts removed, at the scones, the rich clotted cream. Only I notice that with every sip of tea Mrs. Miramontes's face loses a tiny bit more of its color. And only I know why her eyes are darting around as though someone has left a radio on somewhere in the house, and her life depends on her finding it.

"Are you all right, Inés?" Clicky Heels asks, a line scoring between her plucked eyebrows.

"Yes, of course." But I know she's lying. Just like she's lying when she says she'd happily pour Kitty some more tea. When her hands touch the silver pot she looks like she's opened a rattling door in her house and found a side door to Hell. The record's reached its end—Eydie Gormé is done blaming it on the bossa nova and its magic spell—and the room fills with the sound of the needle as it begins to scratch.

"Inés, really—what's the matter?" There's a spike of fear in Clicky Heels's tone.

"They're all of them singing in misery." This is Mrs. Miramontes's voice, but I've never heard her sound like this. Her rounded patrician tones are all gone, stripped away, and what's left is nothing but raw fear and pain. "They cough up silica in their lungs. I can hear them calling to each other. The overseers whip them into the mouth of the mine. It eats men, they say. The mountain eats men."

"Which mountain, darling?" Kitty's teacup is hovering halfway to her mouth. The ladies dart eyes at one another, but none of them move. I wonder if they're afraid it's catching, whatever babbling disease has overtaken their hostess.

"Potosí. They say this mine is the mouth of the devil. They feed the devil their bodies and the mountain belches out silver and blood." She looks as though she's desperate to set down the silver pot, but her hands stay clenched around the handle, gripping it tight.

I slip out before the ladies can see me, and from Violeta's room I can hear Mrs. Miramontes as they usher her into her bedroom, hear them fluttering around her as she protests that she's fine now, it was just a headache. Panic shoots through her voice when someone calls out for Fernanda to ring the doctor. I can feel guilt, like a cold finger on my spine, because I know just what a doctor might do with a woman babbling about hearing voices from Indians in silver mines. *I only wondered how quickly they'd send for the van*, Violeta wrote. I've heard the stories from some of the couch girls, the warnings, about where those vans like to take "degenerates" like us. A woman might enter that van as a person, but she'll leave it as a *mental patient*, and if she doesn't know the difference, she'll find out soon enough.

Then I pass in front of her door, see her lying still and silent, and I think of Violeta, trapped just as still and silent for years. I think about Mrs. Miramontes doing nothing to help, and the cold finger retreats from my spine. The salve jar is in my apron pocket, the smell of it rich and sharp.

Well done, Violeta spells out with her tiles. *When will you do it again?*

I shake my head, a move I regret because it makes the pain radiate through my skull. I've taken four more aspirin, to no effect, and I don't dare take any more.

What?

"It did feel good, okay?" And now that finger is back, prodding at me, the guilt lodging itself in my chest. "And maybe that's the problem. This isn't about helping you, and we both know it."

It helped me.

I bet it did. "You know what I mean."

What if . . . Violeta's little head tilts to one side, for so long that I wonder if the plastic is stuck.

We kept going? We could make her help us. If she's afraid enough.

I don't answer right away. I haven't told her about the pain, or about the guilt wrapping itself around my heart, warring with the warm rush of pride. I invented another spell on my own. A spell that could drive a woman mad and take her freedom away. Just like Violeta lost all of hers. There it is again, the thrill of my old skin shedding itself, of the crackling, dangerous power flowing through my hands.

My mother would have told me to pay attention to my guilt,

to what it was telling me. My grandmother would tell me to make some more special tea, and brew it stronger this time. Doris would say to get the hell out of here before I get myself in any deeper.

"There are things no one deserves. Not even her," I say, when I finally trust myself to speak. I prepare to watch the Scrabble tiles go flying like the planchette did, but Violeta just slides them around, back and forth, like a woman pacing a narrow hall.

"I won't drive her insane. But she doesn't need to know that, does she?"

Dr. Levin rattles up the stairs just after five, right when he promised Fernanda he'd come. I hear scraps of their conversation through the gleaming wood of the door. His voice, strong and patronizing: "Your friends . . . concerned for you . . . hearing voices . . . men who weren't there?" Her voice, struggling not to rise: "Imagination ran away . . . thank you . . . only aspirin and rest." I can hear the fear inside it from here. The hinges of his black bag open wide; he's taking out the tools that until now have probably never made her afraid. You should try being brown, Mrs. Miramontes. Then you'll see how often doctors in white coats are your friends.

I listen for a few minutes more, as his booming tones soften a bit and the sharp fear has drained from her voice. I can hear the instruments slipping back into his bag, her tone almost back to normal now. That's when I knock on the door.

"I heard you weren't feeling well, ma'am, so I brought you

some tea." The smells of bergamot and jasmine rise into the air, the same blend as this afternoon. I don't put it on the bedside table; I hold it right out to her, humming "Amazing Grace" under my breath. She has to thank me and take the mug from my hands, and as soon as it touches her skin I can see her fighting to control the muscles in her face.

"Are you having another episode?" Dr. Levin pulls the notebook back out of his bag, pen poised and ready.

"No, no, of course not. It's just . . . um, perhaps I'll wait a bit, dear."

"I'm sure this will help, ma'am. Don't worry; it's cool enough to drink." The doctor's pen is hovering over the page, and under his gaze she has to lift the mug to her mouth, a mouth that's shaping itself as if to drink poison. He and I both watch the last bit of color drain from her face as she drinks, and as she tries to set down the mug and finds that she can't. Just like in the parlor. Her eyes are screaming now, in a terror she can't let past her mouth. I see him writing in his little notebook: *Obsession with tea.*

"I'm sorry, ma'am—maybe I added too much sugar?" I say. "I'll go down and make some more." And I take it from her with only the tiniest tug.

"Oh, well, thank you so much, dear. But I'm sure Fernanda can take over from here. She'll be staying here tonight; the doctor insisted. Feel free to return to Violeta now."

I make sure to clumsily knock a doily onto the floor as I go, so that I can kneel down and pick it up and hear Dr. Levin say, "I remain concerned, Mrs. Miramontes. I'm going to return tomorrow afternoon. Until then, I must insist that you remain in your bed. If you continue to have episodes, I have a colleague who's a widely respected psychiatrist." Even after I've shut the door, I can hear her demurring and protesting, and his voice booming over hers, overruling her. The net is slipping around her, but she can't feel it yet.

When the clock strikes eleven, when Violeta is back in her body and soundly asleep, and I can no longer hear Fernanda's feet on the stairs, I begin weaving a nightmare. I use more sage, of course, and a few drops of bergamot tea, and a pair of silver earrings from Violeta's childhood room. The thread from that midnight-blue gown. And, in a fit of mischief, a tiny engraving of the devil torn from the family's illustrated Bible, my clumsy scribblings adding a screaming stick figure pouring out of his mouth. Finally, from the record I snagged from the rickety credenza in the parlor, the Everly Brothers' most saccharine hit drifts into the air: "All I have to do is dream . . ."

SEVENTEEN

I wake in the morning with the vise barely loosening its hold. This pain will visit me, then, every time I perform this spell. It will hurt me more every time, and take longer to fade. The price for letting her have my body, taste that freedom, write me letters that send a hot flush down my throat and my thighs. Any movement sends more pain radiating down my arms and legs, through the bones, through the skin. How long will it take to leave me? Will it disappear after Andrés comes back tomorrow and I can finally break the spell, the way the entire castle woke up when Sleeping Beauty did? Or will it stay with me forever, a price I've already signed on for without knowing it? I wonder if this is the real reason my grandmother warned me away from this spell. Or if she's ever actually pulled this off, ever got far enough to know this would happen.

I make myself head down the stairs to the kitchen, wincing slightly at the sun coming through the stained glass. I can't dwell too long on the magic I've already done; there's more of it, waiting for me to do.

When I knock on Mrs. Miramontes's door at eight thirty, she looks shrunken inside her mountain of bedcovers. When I see her face, the icy guilt comes right back, and I'm grateful for it this time. It's the least I deserve, after what I've done to this woman, and what I'm going to do. I turn on her overhead lights, but there's still a darkness in this room that won't fade.

"How are you feeling, ma'am? Forgive me for intruding, but Violeta's physical therapist is here now, and Fernanda is somewhat overwhelmed, so I thought I would bring you a breakfast. Just some poached eggs and toast."

"Overwhelmed? Why? Where is Rosario?"

"I understand that Rosario is quite sick, ma'am." I don't mention that I used the little phone book in the kitchen to call Rosario and tell her all about the possessed tea party, the babbling about silver mines and the mouth of the devil. I could almost hear the frightened woman cross herself over the phone.

"I'll do my best to pitch in, Mrs. Miramontes. Here, I made you some coffee." Not tea, she can tell by the aroma, but all the same, I can see her hands shaking again even before they touch the cup, and the relief practically splashing over her face as nothing happens. Nothing happens, either, as she takes her first sip, or the second, and I walk out of the room.

Of course not. I treated the silverware this time.

"How lovely, dear." Mrs. Miramontes's voice is strained with barely contained impatience at the fact that I keep showing up in her room, this time setting a bowl of soup by her bedside, shutting her curtains against the midday sun. "But Fernanda can do this, can't she?"

I let my forehead score with a worry line and my hands clasp tightly together. "Ma'am, you insisted that Fernanda take the afternoon off. I thought it was very kind of you."

"You must be mistaken, dear," she says. "I'd surely remember if I'd said that." But she's not at all sure. I can tell by the trembling she's trying so hard to control.

"I remember you saying it, ma'am. The doctor had just left. Are you certain you're all right? I'm so sorry; I don't really know what to do. Should I call him? Perhaps he could come even earlier."

Her answer is a fit of coughing. "Of course not; there's no need. I must have just forgotten. Well, I'll ring if I need anything." I nod and set the tray where her bedside telephone used to be. The doctor insisted on taking it away yesterday. "You just focus on getting better," he told her as he wrapped up the cord, and I felt a flash of disgust at him, that little puffed-up tin god, wearing his power in his starched white coat.

But it does make my plan easier. She can't use any of the other phones in the house without disobeying his order to stay in bed, and if she does I'll hear her open the door. She can't just dial Andrés in Switzerland and conspire with him, in whatever way those two conspire together. I make sure the brass bell is within her reach and then leave her alone with her terror. Then I go and close the door to my windowless room and sit in the dark, alone with mine.

There's a border I've told myself I won't cross, that I'll stay inside of, remaining myself. But those lines get real fuzzy when I make myself think about them. Does it matter that I'm not doing any serious harm, just threatening it? That I'm doing this for love, not revenge? (*You sure about that?* Doris would ask.)

And do my reasons even matter if I unleash something I can't control?

And what if I've already crossed that border in the dark, and I don't even know?

Dr. Levin's back for his promised follow-up, and I wait only a few minutes before I knock again on the door, again bearing tea. Mrs. Miramontes begins to shake, this time before she touches the cup, and I watch the doctor's eyes narrow. He turns to me, his face a map of worry lines. "Nati, is it true that your employer dismissed the maid for the afternoon?"

"I've been taking care of her, sir."

He ignores this and addresses the still woman in the bed. "I thought I told you how important it was that you not be left alone."

"Yes, Doctor. I don't . . . I don't know what I was thinking."

He turns back to me. "Has she had any more incidents?"

The line I'm walking is so gossamer-thin, only a spider could feel it.

"Incidents, sir?"

"Yes, young lady. Anything like yesterday afternoon in the parlor."

"I'm so sorry, sir; I wasn't in the parlor yesterday. Violeta needs a lot of attention. But I'm sure Mrs. Miramontes just needs her rest. And maybe some hot liquids. Here, ma'am: We don't want your tea to get cold. Oh, and Doctor, I also made you a cup." I pass him a white mug, which I've filled with the same tea, except not a hint of magic when I made it. He takes a long, healthy draw from it, and now she has no excuse not to pick up hers from the tray.

Dr. Levin's eyes swivel to her face, watching for the slightest hint of a tremor. *Obsession with tea*, he wrote in his notebook yesterday. I don't need to look at her face as she takes it from me, trying desperately to put off drinking it without making his little pen scratch something even worse. I look instead at the mirror above her dresser, the pristine glass like a movie screen. It shows me the instant her hands touch the mug, the one I treated with salve and filled with tea that I brewed in that same silver teapot from yesterday, "Amazing Grace" playing while it steeped.

For an instant, maybe two, she almost makes it. With her first sip, the only sign that anything is wrong is again that last bit of color drained from her face. I lean over to prop up the pillow behind her head. "There. It's doing you better already. Maybe just a few more sips." My eyes are on her, and the doctor's are too, and as soon as she swallows the liquid her mouth contorts into a low wail.

"Why? Why won't it stop? What have I done?" And she tries now to set down the mug, but just as with the teapot, her hands can't seem to release their grip. Her eyes are darting out to mine, to the doctor's, and we both watch as she finally throws it into the corner of the room, her hands left clutching the empty air as the mug shatters against the wall.

Then there's nothing but silence, as I pick up the shards, as the doctor's pen scritches over his notebook. Nothing but a woman's defeated sobs. Finally he speaks.

"Mrs. Miramontes, I must insist that you be evaluated by a

psychiatrist, especially given your history." I pretend not to perk my ears up at this. "If you continue to have episodes, we'll need to discuss what might be the safest place for you. Your son-in-law will return tomorrow afternoon, you said?" She nods, her face tightening.

"Well, when he returns he and I will need to have a long conversation about your well-being. My colleague will be here at noon tomorrow. Here, young lady; take my card. If anything occurs before then, call right away. My service can always reach me." The net is nearly drawn around her. I just have to make sure that she can feel it. I try not to think about how hard it is to control the strands, how if I'm not careful this might end with her being put somewhere I can't pull her out of. Like a white van.

As he's packing up his bag, I pause at the door, and speak, tray in hand. "I'll be back in a little while with some soup, Mrs. Miramontes. And some more tea." Dr. Levin's done with us, zipping up his bag, and he doesn't look at either of us before he thumps down the steps.

~

It's two minutes past midnight when I knock on Mrs. Miramontes's door. Twelve hours before the psychiatrist is scheduled to come; sixteen hours before Andrés returns. Two minutes after the last of the sand has poured through the hourglass, ending her sleeping spell. Every time I've knocked lately I've brought nothing but nightmarish visions and fear, and I think she's beginning to notice. Maybe even ask herself why.

"It's very late, dear." I hear her shaky voice through the door. "Are you all right? Is something wrong with Violeta?"

"Oh, no, ma'am. I just wanted to make sure you woke up all right from your nightmare. This one wasn't too bad, I hope. Not too many devils. Better than last night's, I'm sure."

Utter silence as she realizes I couldn't possibly know about any devils—unless I put them there.

"You and I need to speak, Mrs. Miramontes. If you keep having these terrible visions the doctors might send you away. And I don't think any of us want that. So, let's have a little talk, yes?" The net is entirely thrown over her now. She needs to feel me gather the strands in my fist, to know that I could tighten them anytime I like.

And then she opens her door.

"What do you want from me?"

She's trembling, and I can see how hard she's trying to make her face a smooth mask of indignation, the face she's used to wearing when the help dares to slip out of their role. When she sees me gesture to her daughter's room, her entire body goes taut and still, as if the devil of Potosí himself were waiting inside.

"Relax. It's just your daughter. And what I want is for you to help her. Help us both. Now, come along. I brought you a chair from the parlor." It's the same high-backed, faded thing she sat in yesterday, during Sunday afternoon tea. And her entire body looks like that chair is the mouth to hell.

"Please have a seat, ma'am. I won't offer you any tea. Here, meet your daughter. She might look a little different than usual." I gesture to Violeta, ensconced in the body of the doll, sitting up next to her vacated body, in front of the Ouija and the Scrabble sets. The little plastic hand waves.

"Your daughter has some questions for you. Don't you, Violeta?"

"You're mad. You're insane." She takes a step backward, nearly tripping over her gown.

"I don't think so. Violeta?"

And the doll hand reaches for the Ouija board and begins to form words. Scrabble tiles might be faster, but I appreciate her sense of theatrics.

Just tell me why.

"Please, dear—please, Nati—Natalia—please tell me what is going on here."

"Your daughter asked you a question, ma'am. I think she deserves an answer." I'm almost worried about how good it feels to speak to her this way. It's something I've wanted to do my whole life, to people like her.

When she still says nothing, I walk over to my record player and settle the needle into the groove, the needle I've wrapped in a stolen spiderweb, still thick on my fingers like silk.

If Mrs. Miramontes could doubt or explain away everything before, that's all gone the second the notes of the song swell in the air. From my record player on Violeta's dresser, the Victrola downstairs in the parlor, the little transistor radio in the kitchen, the upright piano in the music room, and the mandolin hanging above it on the wall. All of them with my stolen web woven around them, all of them filling the house with the same tune, the Everly Brothers' most saccharine hit. The one from her nightmares two nights running.

Well? The little hand spells out, tapping on the Ouija board. And Mrs. Miramontes faints.

I always thought fainting women were a cliché of Victorian plays, a relic of the days of chloroform and high-buttoned shoes. But there's an actual jar of smelling salts in the kitchen, Violeta tells me with Scrabble tiles. When I wave them under Mrs. Miramontes's nose, she wakes up, but she looks like she'd like to swallow the entire jar if it could send her away from this room.

"Let's don't have that happen again, shall we?" I tell her. The record player's off now, but I dangle the needle over it, and I can feel that power now, hot and electric, and it feels so easy and natural, flowing through my hands. And there's nothing this lady can do now, nothing else she can do but sit, and confess. To her credit, she doesn't blubber or beg for forgiveness. She just talks. She lets out a long, shuddering breath, as she voices things she's probably never been able to speak.

"Violeta, do you remember that first nurse you had, right after you were . . . stricken? That tiny little thing who sang to you and always wore those long earrings?"

Yes.

"Well, I was very confused when she was gone after something like a week; she'd seemed so dedicated to you. And then it happened again with another nurse, and even that nice young doctor from Panamá. It felt like so many of them just didn't last. Andrés said something about wanting only the best for you, but I started to wonder. At first I thought it was . . . well, just like many men, Andrés never stopped himself from admiring a beautiful woman, and I wondered if some of them had been a bit put off."

I remember Andrés looming over me in the doorway, dressing gown exposing his chest. My nails dig half-moons into my palms.

"Then one day I was in the library, looking for something on the bottom shelf by the door. So when the two of them went into the parlor I don't think they knew I was in there."

Who?

"Andrés and your new physical therapist. She was telling him that she'd found a way for you to communicate with her. By blinking. And he turned into someone I'd never seen before. That smile he wears? It just peeled off his face like it was made of wax. He told her she had no business getting her patient all worked up for nothing, and her family too. He gave her three days' wages and told her to never come back."

Violeta's hand moves over the planchette.

He couldnt ever know. Safer that way.

I'm struck by how clever Violeta has had to be. Andrés thought he'd succeeded in paralyzing her completely; he thought he was in the clear. I imagine the fear and panic that must have simmered behind that smooth face when he heard those people telling him otherwise, and he wondered if he had somehow failed. And then Violeta, trying again and again to reach out, praying that this time a nurse, a therapist, somebody, would tell one of the other nurses about what they saw, instead of telling the one man who needed it not to be true. I wonder how many days, weeks, went by, before she finally realized it was never going to work. And of course Andrés had to hedge his bets, switching out physical therapists, nurses, whenever he felt like it. *Nobody stays long here.*

Outside us, the sky is as black as it ever gets, but now it feels like the darkness is growing even thicker, descending around the three of us like a cloak.

"Of course I was suspicious, but I didn't know anything. I snooped, one afternoon, in Andrés's private study. And that's when I found the spell. He kept it under a desk blotter. It had your name, and a picture of you, and I had no idea what I was seeing, not really, but it made my skin crawl." She recoils, as if her body is remembering.

"And then I was foolish. I was sure it was just some dark superstition, but I knew it meant nothing good, all the same. I forgot all my caution and I ran to Andrés and confronted him. Your father was away on a . . . business trip." I say nothing. The help all know what kind of business he used to do on those trips. And who with.

"You should have seen Andrés at that moment. Smooth as cream. He said that of course he hadn't done a thing to you, Violeta, and that I was hysterical. And then he said, 'But if I did, it was because I had no choice.' Then he told me you had gone to a lawyer, that you had made sure he got nothing if you divorced or if you died. He told me he had been taking out loans for business deals, using your land as collateral, and if he lost those deals, he'd be wiped out. And we'd be wiped out too."

I think of that warning from Violeta, about Andrés needing her.

"Andrés told me that surely you'd be your old self again once he'd closed on his next deal. I shouted at him, called him terrible things. He turned on a dime. He said he was very concerned for your safety, with me babbling about witchcraft and spells.

That afternoon when your father returned he told me to stay out of your room, that Andrés had heard me raving about you being bewitched. He brought in Dr. Levin to deal with me. The same one who came in the first time I caught your father cheating and I became too 'overwrought.' I had to agree to let the doctor sedate me this time too, until I was 'back in control of myself,' as they said."

I can picture it exactly. The three men, polished and calm. One in a white coat, two in black suits, looming over the women in this house, trading their lives like Scrabble tiles. And Mrs. Miramontes, always blurry and soft, always looking distant even when she was right there in the room. She's shivering now, and I pick up one of Violeta's quilts and drape it over her shoulders. In this way, I am my mother's daughter too.

"I was concerned, of course, about your lands being seized if his business deal went south. But it yielded a profit, and we haven't had to sell so much as a square foot of your land. And I kept refilling the prescription. It made everything easier. Eventually I got a . . . a milder dose."

For a moment I can't bear to breathe the same air as the woman across from me. It seems I didn't need to pull the mask off her face; she's showing us herself what's underneath.

So you traded my life for yours, Violeta spells out.

"What would you have had me do? March into some office—a lawyer, a doctor, the police?—saying that my son-in-law was bewitching my daughter? And who would have believed me, when I wasn't even certain I believed it myself? I kept bringing in doctors, until Andrés put a stop to that too. He said it was disturbing your care and getting my hopes up for nothing, and he reminded me that as your husband he was in charge of you. He doesn't even have to keep you here. He would never put you in an institution, not where someone would surely try to communicate with you. But he could take you away from here, where who knows what he'd do to you. He could put *me* in one, where I couldn't even try to protect you."

You mean protect the family.

"You act like that's some trivial thing to care for. You can't appreciate what a responsibility we bear." Her chin points to the portrait in the hall, the one with General Del Valle accepting his land grant. Land that was stolen from the Indians and put into his domain.

"I grew up with that hanging over me my entire life. My great-great-grandfather." She actually shrinks down a tiny bit as she glances up at those painted eyes. "Before I could read I knew that the last of the Spanish colonial governors gave him this land. Before this place was even Mexico, let alone the United States. Our name was once spoken in the same breath as some of the oldest families to settle this place. Peralta, De Anza, Mesa, Del Valle, Amador. And of those hundreds of dignified families, only a few dozen of us have held on. After fighting off coyotes and Indians and disease and God knows what else, building their wealth, our wealth, brick by brick."

I have to stand now, my hands gripping each other, my knuckles white. "Did they build their own wealth, Mrs. Miramontes? Because I think the Indians might have had something to do with it."

"Think what you will about that, young lady. But during the worst harvests, my great-great-grandfather was tilling the same land that his Indian boys did, right by their sides. And when he should have been living out his dignified old years, the gold rush came, and all of a sudden the land became a different country, under his very feet. He spent the last years of his life fighting to defend what was his, from land squatters and speculators and the government itself. Imagine an old man, nearly seventy, traveling all the way to the state capital, only for them to look at his land grants and declare that they weren't valid, because they weren't written in English. By the time he had them translated and notarized and brought back to the courts, half of his lands were gone. You young ladies are spoiled. You've never had to carry the weight of it, all the days of your life." And she slumps down in the chair, this woman whose posture has always been finishing-school perfect.

"The weight of what?" I ask. I already knew how this kind of wealth was a millstone around this family's neck. But I had no idea how heavy it was, how badly it twisted and warped. What must it have been like for her, trying to grow up in this place, carrying all that around?

"Of being the last of my line, and a girl to boot. Taxes kept going up every year, and expenses, and when I was a teenager the Depression came and knocked us further back. My brothers were gone before they turned eighteen: influenza, tetanus. My father didn't even try to hide his disappointment at having only a daughter left: no one to carry on his name, much less find a way to rebuild our fortunes. I was beneath his notice, even though I did what I'd been raised to do and married a wealthy man of Spanish descent. Never mind whether I cared for that man or not." I try to imagine sliding into bed at night with someone whose touch I feel nothing for, and the revulsion shudders down my spine.

"Your father's money was supposed to save us, but he had . . . expensive tastes, shall we say. We've had to sell off more and more of what should have been your birthright, Violeta. Soon enough it will all be gone. These Americans look at us and they think we're no better than the pitiful wretches who swim over to this country to scrub floors. Who else will show them they're wrong?"

How quickly she's forgotten I'm here. I'm back to being invisible. Whatever sympathy I was beginning to feel for her, she's punched it down with a manicured fist. I cross the hallway and knock the framed ancestor onto the floor.

"My mother scrubbed your floors, you miserable wretch. And you're not even fit to shine her boots. You never were." I didn't decide to go stand over her chair. I just did it. I'm not sure where careful, thoughtful Nati has gone, but she's nowhere in this room.

"Do you remember what you people did when my mother got sick? You fired her for taking too many days off. You know, days off to go visit the doctor. And then when she died you sent me a card. Just a week's pay inside, the least of what you owed her. You want me to show you now who's pitiful? Is that what I should do?" I can't remember the last time I raised my voice like this to someone, and never, ever to someone I worked for. My face is hot, my hands clenched again into fists, and now the fists are clenching the pale blue cloth on the dresser, the cloth that's only inches from her face. I remember my mother ironing these blue folds, the hot metal burning her hands. I can practically feel the heat now, burning through my own fists. I could probably think up a spell that could summon that heat and bring it right into this room.

There's a tug at my sleeve. Violeta. She's spelling out something now, tile by tile. On the chair, Mrs. Miramontes is looking at me, her eyes wide and terrified. There's a mirror above the dresser, but I don't need to look into it to see what my face has become. I can just look into hers. Below me Violeta has spelled something out with the tiles. She hasn't written *what are you doing* or *please stop*. She's not afraid of the darkness coursing through me, beating inside my chest. She's written just this: *Keep control.* Reminding me to make sure I'm the one wielding the darkness, not the other way around. Yes, Doris, I have fallen in love with this girl. I make myself breathe a long, slow breath, make my hands unclench, before I speak again.

"You can kick me out tomorrow, Mrs. Miramontes. You can even find some excuse to have me thrown in jail. It won't matter. Those nightmares, those visions, are still going to come for you." That's not quite true, but she doesn't know that, any more than she knows I have no intention of actually sending her to a mental ward. "Unless you help me. I came here to free your daughter, since apparently you can't. And you're going to help."

"You are barking mad. And you're foolish. Just what do you think I can do? He's more devious than you can imagine. For years he's had me right where he wants me. And Violeta too."

"Oh, really?" I say. "Do you think he'd want all three of us here, talking, in this room? All three of us united on one thing, and only one thing—how much we hate him?"

The crumpling, tear-soaked layers of her face look no less

pathetic than they ever did. But I can see a few other layers fighting to emerge. Deviousness, and a flash of hope, and behind all of that a simmering hatred of Andrés. Not nearly as strong or as useful as Violeta's, because Mrs. Miramontes is still a monster at her core. One who cares more about status and propriety and long-dead ancestors than she cares for her living daughter. But she may just be a useful monster now.

"We're going to start with where you found that spell, Mrs. Miramontes."

"He might have moved it. He might have burned it."

One way to find out, Violeta spells with her tiles. *Go.*

I come along, of course, with the little blond doll on my hip, so Violeta can see. Mrs. Miramontes's hand shakes as her skeleton key opens the master suite, making sure that nothing touches the polished doorknob but the sleeve of her gown.

The second the door opens I feel that eerie prickle up the back of my neck. This place is all emerald satin and polished wood, and so scrubbed it's almost sterile. Everything on the dresser, the bedside table, is laid out at exactly ninety degrees. My hands are itching with the desire to steal, and while Mrs. Miramontes is urging the heavy iron skeleton key through the door of his study I open a drawer with the hem of my gown, and I pluck a thread from one of his monogrammed handkerchiefs. Then I hear Mrs. Miramontes call me over to his walnut desk, a piece of white paper in her hand.

"He never even moved it," she's saying, incredulous. "Such arrogance to think I'd never come looking for it again. Or maybe he knew full well that I could take it to *The New York Times*, for all it mattered." She's holding it out to me now, a simple rectangular card, like the ones women use to write down their recipes. It's covered in a thin, looped handwriting, the black ink fading to gray.

It's my grandmother's handwriting.

EIGHTEEN

I knew. I knew who she was, long before I ever knocked on her door. I knew it on that first visit when I was thirteen, when Grandma made the spider strangle itself. I saw that in my nightmares for nights on end. The web was strung with rows of baby teeth, biting.

I knew on my second visit a week later, when she took in my pale face and the black circles under my eyes and smirked. "How've you been sleeping, little girl?" I said nothing and she said nothing and then she pulled up a chair and began teaching me how to make ants dance the mambo across the dining room floor. At lunchtime she fed me Campbell's soup and then she looked at me and poured down a tiny shot of something candy-apple red and streaked with black. The second she swallowed it her spine contorted and her mouth opened so wide it looked like her jaw had disconnected, and her entire throat was that shiny red. I shrieked, stumbling backward until I felt the door at my back, and I scrambled for the doorknob. She leaned in close to my face and howled. Then she opened that red mouth even wider and howled again, a low and guttural sound that made the windowpane shiver in its cheap frame.

"That's a screaming potion," she said, after I had stopped crying and we were both back at the table, my soup grown cold. No apologies, nothing but pride on her face. "It feeds on fury, and anything else it likes to use. When I decide you're ready I'll teach you how to make it. Today's version came out especially good, don't you think?"

I knew then. I just chose to ignore it, so I could keep coming back, keep telling myself the fairy tale where I was the young sorceress denied her birthright, and my grandmother the wise old sage, connecting me to the powers awaiting me in my blood. I was foolish. I was thirteen.

My mother didn't know about those visits to the dark little apartment on Adeline Street, not right away. But then she found the finger of bone, which I'd dropped behind my bed, and the crushed sage. And she put it together with my nightmares and the dark circles under my eyes and the way I wouldn't look at her before I left the house that morning. I'd never kept secrets from her before.

That Sunday, my third visit, and my last, I heard steps pounding up the porch, and Grandma's door slammed open with such force it left its imprint on the wall. And there was my mother, standing in the open doorway. Grandma was singing along with Sammy Davis Jr.'s voice from her record player—"That Old Black Magic"—and I was pulling shadows out of the corners, their forms glistening, dotted with teeth.

"Natalia. You need to come home with me now."

I didn't take my eyes off the shadows; they were slippery and loose, and kept trying to escape my grip. They reminded me of playing with mercury.

"Natalia. Please. You don't know what you're doing. She's got you unleashing things you can't control."

My grandmother stood and crossed to her wall of records. "Actually, Jovita, your girl seems to know very well what she's doing. She'll be very formidable, given half the chance. Who are you to deny her that?"

"I know what you'd turn her into. A little version of you, just like you tried to do with me. Natalia, listen. Your grandmother doesn't care who gets hurt, as long as she gets a good spell out of it."

"Those spells kept you and your sister fed and clothed," my grandmother said, plucking a tiny framed photo from the windowsill. Now she smeared something stinking and horrible on the glass, and an Etta James song crackled from her record player. My mother crumpled onto the ground, hands scrabbling blind on the floor.

"Your eyes are still there," my grandmother assured her. "But illusions are more powerful than you know."

"Stop it, Grandma!" I dropped my hands to my sides and ran to my mother, and the shadows leapt for the ceiling, flashing their teeth. Two of them swirled into each other, and now they were a black cloak, hovering over my mother and me. I tried to pull one back under the windowsill, but it darted out at me, hissing past my face. I knew that this spell was thick with illusions, that the teeth couldn't be real, but that meant nothing as they barely missed my vein.

"Make them stop!" I screamed.

Grandma just smiled and pointed with her chin. "You've got some powerful shadows, little girl. They're beautiful to watch."

The shadow cloak hovered over me, enormous and dark, glistening. Grandma waited, eyes on me. A stream of sunlight peeked through her blinds.

Light could battle shadow, couldn't it? I crawled to the kitchen, with its simple, ordinary things: a vinyl tablecloth, a sink with a flounced curtain hiding Fabuloso cleaner, Comet scrub. And a wooden box of candles, the paraffin kind.

"Grandma. Light me a match." Her expression said she'd been waiting for just that command, and the ring of flame flickered over her face. I lit the candle and stuffed it into an empty wine bottle and stood, and the shadows fled into the corner, cowering. My grandmother grinned. The cloak tried to unknit itself but I was too fast, and I stood on the coffee table and held the flame to the glistening teeth. The shadow howled and hissed and burned away, black mist settling over our heads.

"Well done, little girl." And then Grandma whispered something over the tiny framed photograph, humming, and my mother stood again, and when she spoke her voice was edged in steel.

"If you come near my daughter again, I'll kill you." And she reached out her hand and I took it and walked out the door, barely remembering to grab my satchel and my sweater. I wanted nothing of mine in that place.

~

On the way home my mother let me cry and cry, but she held up her hand when I tried to apologize, instead pulling over at an empty park overlooking Sausal Creek.

"We're long overdue for a talk, Natalia, about some things

that I've kept from you. And about why." But she didn't speak, just sat, waiting, playing with the loose cloth on the fraying driver's seat. Mom never fidgeted. Finally I spoke.

"What did you mean, about Grandma trying to make you into a little version of her?"

Two of the threads pulled away in her hands.

"It started when we were very small. We'd help her gather things. At first it seemed harmless, because she made and sold lots of ordinary things. We'd gather aloe for burn salves, prickly pear for jellies and jams. Stuff like that. As we got older the items got scarier, and so did she. And she started hinting what she was really up to. Slowly. Once she could trust us not to blab. When I was only a little younger than you, it became my job to gather objects at night." Three more threads came away, and now she was pulling another, a habit she'd always told me was shortsighted and destructive.

"The strange thing, Natalia, is that those nights shaped me, all right, but maybe not the way she intended. See, there I'd be, with my one little lantern, so terrified, and the only way to calm my fear was to notice everything. A twig would snap and I'd jump half a foot, and it would turn out to be a scared little rabbit. That's how I learned that the world is full of things that seem daunting, until you pay attention. Nature is; workplaces are too. Hognose snakes that puff themselves up but then roll over and play dead. Bosses that puff themselves up and talk a big game but then roll over and give in when ten coworkers line up outside their door."

And then Mom's hands were back in her lap, quiet and still.

"But what your grandmother does is the opposite of that.

She's got spells that seem innocuous but that escape your grip and do damage you can't undo. Or that summon things that she promises will be only illusion but that really bite, really draw blood. Blood she'll find some way to use for her next spells, perhaps. Apparently terror makes a fantastic ingredient."

And I stared at her shoulder, bare in her sleeveless blouse, and that raggedy scar, what I could now see as a bite mark, from teeth that must have been strong and sharp. And not human.

"Your grandmother doesn't care what she unleashes, Natalia. Or who gets hurt."

"All she cares about is making money," I said, slumped down in the seat.

"Not quite. Let me put it this way. . . . It felt good, wielding the powers she was teaching you. Didn't it?"

"Yes," I admitted, after half a minute went by.

"Well, that's what she cares about. It changes a person. She started with just a few spells, to help pay the bills. Then a few more, and then a few more. I saw what it did to her. She was never a kind person, exactly, but it made her worse than she ever was. To the point where she was no longer the woman your tía Soledad and I knew. You're a good person, Natalia. Don't you want to stay that way?"

I nodded, my cheeks still damp.

"Then throw that spell box away." And I opened my door, the box in my hand. I was shocked at how easy it was, how quickly I stood and tipped the black tin into the muck. A squirrel pawed at it and then recoiled, a faint singe on its fur.

I didn't say a word when we got home and she got out her belt. It was only the second time she'd ever used it on me. I was even glad when the buckle grazed the skin at my waist, drawing blood, a wound I refused to bandage or dress. Let it scab over and scar, I thought. A permanent reminder of how close to danger I'd come.

The scab was still fresh four days later, when I stole back to the creek and retrieved the tin from the mud.

~

The tin is sitting next to me now, on the seat next to a pink-cheeked blond doll, her hair waving in the breeze from the open window of a pearl Cadillac. Behind us in the Orinda hills, Mrs. Miramontes is sleeping, though without any bad dreams woven in this time. She'll wake in forty-three minutes, at eight a.m. sharp. She's afraid of me and she doesn't trust me, which means I can't trust her. Not alone in the house. So she's sleeping, and out of my way.

The freeway exit is half a mile from my grandmother's apartment on Adeline Street. I haven't thought about what I'll do if she's moved, but then I pull up to her building and see her ancient Chevrolet parked at the curb.

NINETEEN

My grandmother doesn't even blink when she opens her door to see me standing there in the morning light, a leather bag at my feet and rage clenching my jaw and my fists.

"I knew it was a matter of time before you came back, little girl. Although, I admit, I thought you'd have come a few years ago."

"You mean when my mother died? Is that your way of saying you're sorry for my loss?"

"Somehow I don't think you're here to talk about her."

"No." And I take the index card out of my pocket, the one with my grandmother's handwriting. She doesn't startle, or ask where I got it. She just glances at the faded ink and then steps back into the house.

"Come in."

The place looks exactly the same as in my memories, except smaller. There's that same fading green couch with an orange afghan, and a knitting bag on the coffee table. *I am a harmless widow*, this decor says. I toss the index card on the table but I don't sit. It's 7:19. Forty-one minutes left, says my watch.

"I want to hear about the man you sold this spell to. Six years ago."

"Ah, yes. Handsome man. Cold and polished. Butter wouldn't melt in his mouth." I grimace, but she doesn't notice.

"You didn't even ask him who the spell was for, did you? Never even thought about it again."

"What good would that do me?" I see a flash of pity on her face, for naive little me.

"His wife is trapped inside her body, did you know that? He's kept her that way for six years. He cheated on her and she went to divorce him and that's what he did to her."

"Pity. I know what awful husbands are like. Not my problem." She sits and picks up her knitting.

I hold up the recipe card. "You have to help me undo the spell you made. This is your writing. This is your doing."

"So?"

Her knitting needles begin clacking, the wool forming a raspberry-colored twin of the afghan on the couch. For a very long moment, I can do nothing but watch the needles weave and weave. She glances up at me, as if to ask why I'm still here.

I push through her beaded curtains to the kitchen and pour a jelly glass of water. It's a pretense, but I gulp it down anyway, splashing a few drops on my shirt. There's a little gray spider scurrying away under the table. Just like the one I used to imagine plotting revenge for the murder of its sister. How many has she sacrificed since then? I pull away a few abandoned strands of its web, rubbing them between my hands.

"Do you like Leonard Cohen, Grandma?" I don't, but I went out a few times with this woman, Ariel, who did. Ariel taught me the lyrics to "Sisters of Mercy," her favorite song, and as I summon one spider, and then another, I sing, low and off-key, about those sisters not departed, not gone. And I add, in a whisper: "Bring me your sisters." A pair of spiders trickles in from under the front door, and now they're pouring in from the cracks in the floor, from the ceiling, through a tiny gap in the wood, weaving their web as they come. They're dust-colored and the size of my thumbnail, and there are so many it's as though I've summoned every one of them that's ever lived—or died—anywhere near this place. They cover the kitchen floor, the cabinets, the walls, webs humming, ready for my command.

"What are you doing, little girl?" That's not exactly fear in her voice, but it's close enough.

"I'm not a little girl. And you need to help me undo that spell you made." Now I move my hands, like I so clumsily did with those shadows, but these creatures are happy to obey my commands, and they glide over the living room floor, over the couch, pulling in lost strands of webs from the corners and threads dangling from her couch, surrounding her faster than she can move. Like a thousand tiny little Shelobs, hot with revenge. Their webs are weaving into each other now, a gossamer twin of her knitted afghan, pulling at her legs and her feet, and she grabs at her knitting, stabbing with her needles at the web. Big mistake: It just weaves itself through the raspberry wool, still wrapped around her fingers, and now her hands are tangled in a web that's suddenly twice its size, and the web is moving over her entire body, and I can hear, low and off-key, the same tune that I sang to them, thrumming through the web as it weaves.

"I've got some powerful spiders here, don't I, Grandma?

They're beautiful to watch." She doesn't squirm or fight; she just stares, waiting to see what I'm going to do. When I whisper to the net, "Time to stop," they leave her trussed, nothing free but her head and her neck.

"Madre de Dios, girl. You're a prodigy. I said you were going to be formidable, but I had no clue. You'll be better than me, given a little training."

"I think I already am." I pluck Violeta from the bag and set her on the coffee table, pink-cheeked and pigtailed and blinking at Grandma with her blue glass eyes.

"What's that?" Grandma recoils as if I'd just put a gris-gris in front of her. "Is that my death?"

"That's Violeta. It was her husband you sold the spell to. He used it on her. For six years, she's only been able to breathe and to blink. A lot like you, right now, except you can still talk. Being inside a doll isn't much of an improvement, but she'll take what she can get."

"You . . . don't mean to tell me that's a real girl's spirit inside that thing?" The blond head nods, and Grandma's mouth drops open. She's forgotten, for a second, to be scared. "No one's ever pulled that one off. Not even me." I want to ask if anybody but me ever thought of asking for permission first, but I don't need to give her any ideas.

"So she's here for revenge, is that it?" Grandma asks.

I can feel the entire web thrumming, eager for my command. *It felt good, wielding the powers she was teaching you. Didn't it?* my mother said, the warning thick in her voice.

"We didn't come for revenge, Grandma. We're here for the key to break a spell."

"I don't believe you."

"Try me." I hold up the index card in front of her face, and I read the last line, in her looped handwriting: *Last, add a drop of the key. This will lock your victim inside.* "Tell me what this key is, Grandma, and where to find it. Then see if you're still breathing when you're done. And hurry. We're going to run out of time." I see Violeta's glass eyes, turned up to me, and if a doll face could express awe, hers would be showing it.

"All right, lit—all right, girl. What have you tried so far?"

As quickly as I can, I explain the reversal spell that didn't work, and the bracelet around Violeta's wrist, a twin of the one around Andrés's neck. We have thirty-one minutes left.

She gives out a low whistle. "That man's a diabolical one, all right. I didn't tell him to swap those things out—he must have thought of that later. So that even I couldn't undo my own spell." She coughs. "I would never have guessed that. But you, girl, you're pretty sharp yourself. You're quite the opponent, aren't you?" I could say that the begrudging respect in her tone is just to soothe me so I'll call off my eight-legged minions. But I'd like to think that it's real.

"The key, girl, is his last bit of insurance. Only he and I know what it is." Immobilized or not, she's enjoying herself as she draws this moment out. "It's a drop of his own blood. And somehow I think you'll be able to wrestle down your conscience to harvest it, yes?" She's speaking to me, but Violeta's eyes swivel toward Grandma, and the plastic head moves up and down. *Yes.* And Grandma grins.

I whisper to the humming web: "Go home now, until I call you again. Unweave all this, and harm no one, and go."

Grandma's face floods with shock she's not even trying to control, as the web begins to free her shoulders, as the little Shelobs skitter away.

"You know, Mom read *Lord of the Rings* to me when I was eleven," I tell Grandma, her face trying to work out why she's still alive. "Every night before bed. She liked to quote Gandalf; he was one of her favorites. 'Do not be too eager to deal out death in judgment.' My mother's gone, but I still have that book. I still have those words. I could have killed you, yes. But, to ask a question you always said was boring: Why should I?"

My grandmother never bothered to ask herself what a spell or a potion was for, never thought about what happened once the money was in her hand and the door shut. It's only about whether she'll manage to invent that new spell, make this salve a bit stronger than last time. The only questions she's ever asked herself are *Can I do this?* Never *should I*, much less *why*. Maybe that's good enough for Grandma, but I am my mother's daughter, and that's not good enough for me. I hold up my hands, feeling that sweet rush of power, and inside it a current of something else, thrumming low and quiet: the satisfaction of going right to the brink, and choosing the moment I will turn back. I take it in, that feeling of power that I will keep there, waiting for when I decide to unleash it, and for the right reason. Like freeing a damsel or two.

"How do you know I won't try to destroy you the second I'm free?" Grandma says, her shoulders freed now, her upper arms peeking through.

"I don't." She flinches as I reach over and pull her clip-on earrings away from her ears, a pair of gold squares around a center of opal. And then I find that same photo she used ages ago, still on the windowsill. It's of my mother, my grandmother, and my tía Soledad, all three of them back in El Paso. Before they boarded the bus to come here. I tuck all of it into my bag, along with Violeta. "Just in case," I tell Grandma, the web nearly down to her elbows, her arms nearly free, and I shut the door and take us away from this place.

TWENTY

I park the Cadillac, quietly, in the garage, and I use the service entrance at the side of the house to sneak inside through the kitchen. The house is silent, the grandfather clock not yet striking eight. I set the bag at my feet, gently, to not jostle Violeta, and into it I slip a paring knife and a shallow bowl, to catch the blood. After a second, I take the tiniest tool in the drawer—I think it's for crabmeat—and drop it into the bag. It's little enough to fit Violeta's hand. Maybe. Six minutes left, says my watch.

"Hello, Nati." I whirl around and there is Andrés, pointing a gun straight at the center of my chest.

"But you don't get here until this afternoon," I stammer, probably the most useless thing I could say while staring down a gun.

"I took an earlier flight. And I'm so glad I did. Imagine my horror when I find my wife practically comatose, and her dedicated caregiver nowhere to be found. And then my mother-in-law, terrifyingly deep in sleep. So naturally I tried this, at her bedside." He gestures at a tiny crystal bowl on the counter behind him. It's filled with water, two blossoms floating on the surface, but these black and shriveled things look like someone's been toasting them under a flame.

"I think you know what this is, Nati. A test anyone, even I, can perform. Now, I knew that there's no way this could be Rosario's doing; that woman can't walk into a room without crossing herself." I've been an atheist all my life, but even I bristle at the contempt in his voice. "Then I thought it might be Fernanda, but she's never been what we'd call clever. And then I realized that you looked familiar. You were that sullen little thing skulking around when I first came to this house, weren't you?"

"Yes." There's no point in lying to him now, at least not about this.

"What a secret you've been keeping. That's all right; I've got secrets of my own. I've actually got to thank you. My wife's even more useful to me in this state than she was before."

"Then why the gun?" I glance up at the kitchen clock. Three minutes left until Mrs. Miramontes wakes up.

"Oh, the gun is for you, of course. And was that some kind of sleeping spell you had for my mother-in-law? That was my guess, when I saw the hourglass. I turned it back. We've got plenty of time." My legs want to tumble underneath me, but if I get any closer to the floor, I might draw Andrés's eyes to the black bag under the table at my feet.

"If you shoot me, what are you going to tell the police?" I've seen enough movies to remember this rule: *Keep them talking.* I know just how much men like him need to brag, especially around women, who he's always been able to control. And I also know what time Rosario's scheduled to be here: eight fifteen, but she's early a lot.

"Nati, I thought you were clever. Look around you. Keys in your hand to the Cadillac you were trying to steal; the silver drawer already open. All I have to add is you ranting about magic and witchcraft"—he points the gun at the dead blossoms—"and they'll close their little notebooks and pat me on the back."

"Are you sure they will?" I'm officially stalling him now, listening for the sound of Rosario's key in the lock. Instead, both Andrés and I jump as the service bell rings.

Rosario's husband looks a lot like a male version of her: small, wrinkled, and worried, the kind who'd sooner wash their own mouth out with soap than say a mean word or tell a lie. He introduces himself to us—he doesn't notice that Andrés keeps his hands inside the pockets of his green cardigan, gripping the gun—and explains that he's come for Rosario's things and to collect her last wages. "My wife is very sorry, but she's concluded that this place is not the best for her." I see him stop himself from reaching for the cross at his neck. Andrés opens his mouth, but I interrupt him. I'm betting an awful lot on the idea that he wouldn't shoot this gentle old man.

"Of course, sir. Mrs. Miramontes instructed me that Rosario might be moving on, and that I was to give her her last wages. Three months' worth, I was told," I lie, smooth as cream. My eyes dare Andrés to contradict me as I open the cabinet by the kitchen door and pull out an envelope. It's the petty cash, for paying delivery people, and I count out the twenties now with a speed that stuns them both. Rosario's husband looks like he wants to say something, but now Andrés claps a patronizing hand on his shoulder and steers the man out the door. "Tell your wife that we were more than satisfied with her work," he says as the service door shuts.

"I take it back, Nati. You're eminently clever. It's a shame you're not on my side." Andrés's hand taps at the gun in his pocket, not yet retrieving it. He might not need to, his body language says; his head towers a foot over mine, his shoulders broad and strong, ready to dole out whatever damage he decides to inflict.

And that's when a crabmeat fork stabs into his Achilles' heel.

If I don't live through the next few minutes, at least I'll die having seen the expression on this cruel, privileged man's face when he realizes this attack came from a twelve-inch-high doll swinging a tiny fork, staining his forty-dollar socks with his blood. He tries to recover, but he's already making mistakes. He kicks at her, but plastic dolls can't feel pain, and she keeps stabbing away. He fumbles for the gun in his pocket, even while her little hand swings again and again, and just as his hand touches the trigger she connects with his tendon, and he doubles over in pain. He drops the gun on the floor, where it spins like a roulette wheel, and when he dives for it, which I predicted he would do, my sneaker connects with his forehead and he drops to his knees, clapping a hand over his left eye, where the salty blood is trickling in, leaving him half blind. He's trying to wipe the blood away and grab for the gun and kick at the stabby doll all at once. And now he's brought more of his body within Violeta's reach, and six years' worth of fury pours through a tiny plastic hand armed with a silver fork.

"Nati! Call that thing off!" he screams, without a hint of irony, as the points of the fork connect with his calf, then his thigh, while the blood is still trickling into his eye. He uses his right sleeve to wipe it away, and again he's fumbling, with no plan; he should have used his left hand for that, leaving his dominant hand to grab for the gun. Because now I can plant my foot firmly on the barrel of the gun, and he knows that he has lost. He looks up at me, fighting to control the pain on his face.

"You need to call off that thing." Bloodied, half-blinded, disarmed, and he's still trying to issue commands.

"That . . . thing?" I point to Violeta. "What, you don't recognize your wife?" He lifts his bloody gaze and stares, at her baby-blue dress stained with red. And with another flash of theatrics that makes my heart swell, she lifts her crab-fork-wielding hand and she . . . she waves.

And now, as I pick up the gun, an idea springs to me, as quick and simple as if I'd pulled it from the walls themselves. I remember the song that played on my grandmother's record player on that last visit, before my mother thundered through the door. "That old black magic . . ." I sing to the man prostrate below me, and I kneel in the shadows on the floor, whispering to them, and they swell in my hands, swirling over his face, and he shrieks and scrabbles away.

"Don't let those things touch you, Andrés," I say, and I grab the black bag from the kitchen and put the gun into the cookie tin treated with my blood. Now it's locked away from him, and anyone else. I wrap a towel around the cookie tin, to protect Violeta from touching it, and slip her inside the bag, little hand still clutching the bloody fork.

The shadows are straining to escape my grip, but I push them at Andrés, chasing him up the stairs. I have to focus on nothing else: not the bloodied man stumbling away from me, not the scratching sound from the parlor, where the ancient Victrola starts itself up and "That Old Black Magic" fills the air. Did one of those shadows escape without me noticing, and start up their own song? *She's got you unleashing things you can't control,* said my mother, years ago. The tune crackles from the little radio in the kitchen, the piano in the music room, and even my own pink record player. This is Frank Sinatra's version, a record this family doesn't even own.

"Do you even know what you're doing?" Andrés asks, as one of the shadows rushes past my face, sending me cowering. "Are you trying to destroy us both?" He's trying to sound indignant, in charge, but I can practically taste his fear as the song rises louder, surrounding us.

He's right, of course. None of this was in my plan. He was supposed to be sleeping, thoroughly, in his own bed, while I stole the bracelet from him and freed his wife and fled with her in her little blue car. It's no help to wonder what my grandmother would do; she'd have killed him already. He's nearly reached the top of the stairs, where he hopes he can close himself off against me and what I've unleashed. I let two of the shadows bleed into each other, and they rush for him, a wave of black.

"Inés! Help me! Call the police!"

"I'm sorry; she can't. The doctor took her phone away. She's been acting very strangely for days. And anyway, didn't you tell me you turned over the hourglass? So she'd sleep even longer?" He's starting to shake. This man of silver cuff links and shined leather shoes, now dragging his injured leg, his bloody eye half swollen, cowering at teeth that aren't really there. He calls out again, though he has to know it won't work: "Inés! For God's sake, wake up! She's insane!"

"Even if she did wake up, you think she would help you? Didn't you try to throw her into a mental ward?" It's so delicious, watching his face collapse as he realizes how all the bridges around him are nothing but ash. He scrambles into his bedroom, and I can see him fumbling at the door to his private study, where there's a telephone.

"You keep your study door locked, right? If it's your key you're looking for, I stole it. I do that sometimes." And I pat the lump of the skeleton key in my pocket. He howls and picks up something from his dresser—it looks like an ashtray—and throws it through the open door, aiming for my face. I duck, and now the shadows pull away from my grip. They swirl around the darkened light fixtures, and then there's a shattering pop and a light bulb falls in glass shards onto the hallway rug. Then another, down the hall, and then two more, as if they've tasted the broken glass and found it good. And now there's nothing between me and Andrés except for ten stairsteps, a narrow hallway, and a lot of empty air.

"I told you, Nati. You haven't thought this through." He tries to smirk, but the fear is still thick on his face, making his mouth an ugly snarl. He takes more shaking steps back toward the staircase again, back toward me. Wincing in pain, moving slowly, but still moving, ducking now as a shadow darts out for his face, broken glass glistening in its teeth. These shadows aren't supposed to be capable of breaking glass. They must be feeding on the magic that's humming all through this house, and I have no idea what they can do, what they'll become. One of them rushes from the ceiling, teeth coming within an inch of my throat.

I shriek and grab the railing, the one that should have been fixed years ago, and I nearly pull the loose, wobbling thing away from the wall, and the bag drops at my feet. The bag where the cookie tin rests, firmly shut. Another shadow swirls at Andrés, and he stumbles, but he recovers, and he keeps coming toward me, back down the stairs. He's eight stairsteps above me, and then I back down two more steps, and now it's ten. And while my feet are moving, my hands are fumbling at the lid of the cookie tin, and I don't dare look down to see what I'm doing. I don't know what I'll do once I open it—I'm not going to send him dancing up the steps, or paint his lips blue.

Then, there it is. From inside the bag, Violeta is shoving something in my direction, an object she heard me describe in full detail only a few hours ago. A tiny vial of something candy-apple red and streaked with black. I know perfectly well I didn't put that thing in my bag. Grandma must have, when I was in the kitchen, plotting a spiders' revenge. It could be poison. Or it could be her twisted attempt at redemption, from a woman who has no idea what that word even means. Or maybe just her idea of a joke.

He's three steps above me now. I open my mouth and swallow it down.

My head drops back, my mouth opens wide, and out of it pours every bit of fury I've ever swallowed in my life. Every time one of the men at the bank "accidentally" brushed up against me; this family's horrible bigotry I had to listen to, with a straight face; every time I watched them talk to my mother as though she knew nothing at all. That never-ending day when I watched her machines grow silent and I felt her hand go slack. It all howls out of my red throat as I advance toward Andrés, and if the power I've felt before was intoxicating, this feels like I could burst through the wood and the walls of this house, my entire body just a thundering scream.

When I come back to myself, his door is shut against me and I hear his whimpering cries as he tries to break down the door to his study to get to the telephone. I urge the skeleton key through the lock of his bedroom door and he shrieks, stopping when he realizes I'm only locking him in.

If anything would have awakened Mrs. Miramontes, that would have done it, but I hear nothing at all from her door. My legs are trembling as I pull each shadow back under my control, feeling them strain against my grip, like wayward children. I send each of them back to their corners, praising them for their service, and as they do I swear I hear a sighing "thank you." Thanking me for the chance to play with music, maybe, or taste broken glass. I'd really rather not think about it too much. I force my weak legs along the hallway and down the stairs, to clean up the blood and the glass, and as the blood disappears, the music softens and dies. The house no longer feels humming with magic; it's like the walls are holding their breath. Waiting, like the web did, for my next command. I need to get us the hell out of here. Fernanda will be here soon, just after nine.

Now it's time. I put Violeta back in her body and from the

back of the freezer I retrieve the picture of her, the one I wrapped in a dark cloth last night and placed here, making sure to use no herbs, whisper no words, sing no songs. The ice is thicker than last time; it'll take longer to thaw. The sand for Mrs. Miramontes's sleeping spell is pouring through the hourglass, nearly gone. All I hear of Andrés is a faint weeping on his side of the door.

I start to mix up a sleeping spell for Andrés, and then I look at Violeta in her bed, this body she's been trapped in for six years, because of this man. So I retrieve the mousetrap from its hiding place and I take their wedding picture, the one where I already tore Violeta from her husband's side, and I slide him between the metal prongs of the trap. Then I remember the thread I stole from his own handkerchief, and I thread a needle with it, my own lips twitching in joy as I sew his mouth shut. The only hourglass I have left is from an old board game, and it will give me five minutes, no more. Five minutes of him trapped, immobile, mute, and awake, while I stand over him and harvest his blood.

I have no idea what I'll do with him after I've taken it, once he regains control. He's a snake, soon to regain the use of his fangs. But I can't make myself think one second more. I take the tiny crabmeat fork, just the right size, the right weight. It's already warm as I slip it in my pocket, as if it's craving more blood. At his door I fumble, and I swear out loud as the skeleton key clatters on the wood floor, and my trembling fingers pick it back up and slide it through the lock. Everything in my body is begging me to let it rest. So close now. I even murmur it to myself: "It's almost over. He's helpless now. Get it done."

Then I smell something familiar, something like old roses, and there's a heavy, sharp thing poking into my back. It's small, I can tell, but it's enough to end everything, with what I need only ten feet away.

"Don't go through that door. Dear."

I turn around, slowly. If she's going to stab me, she's going to have to look me in the eye while she does.

"You were supposed to be sleeping."

"Oh, I've been awake for a while, dear. I've been listening. To everything. My son-in-law is very loud, isn't he? I wonder what happened with your little sleeping spell. Maybe that hourglass extension trick only works for the one who cast it. What do you think?"

"Maybe. Listen, Mrs. Miramontes, everything I need to save your daughter is on the other side of that door." I pull the spell from my pocket, ever so slowly. "He's been holding the key this whole time. It's the bracelet around his neck, and it needs . . . a drop of his blood." I can't believe I'm confiding in her, but it's not like I have much of a choice.

"You want to practice more witchcraft on her?"

"If you want to call it that, go ahead. Please; we only have four minutes. You need to let me finish this now." My watch ticks in the silence. "You can't possibly be here to stop me, can you?" I know how much she craves normalcy, order, no matter how horrendous that order might be. But she has to know that there's no "normal" she can find her way back to. Not now.

"You're in love with my daughter. Aren't you?"

"Yes," I tell her, not looking at the blade pointed at my ribs.

I look at her. At her face, at the whole world war of emotions running across it.

"I thought so," she says. "I could practically smell it. You say you love her, and yet what can you ever give her? Say what you will about the choices I made, but I've always made sure Violeta had a home to live in and a future assured. You can't give her either of those. You can't give her marriage or children. And do you have any idea how the world is going to treat the two of you? How can you possibly give my daughter enough to make up for all that?"

"I think she might like to decide those things for herself, you shrunken ghoul." I should know better than to provoke a woman with her wild eyes and a fistful of steel. But I have no interest in stopping myself.

"And you believe she loves you?" she asks me, her face reflected in the blade of the knife.

"Yes."

"Don't you realize she'll say anything to get out of that bed? Let's see what happens when she's out of it, and all you have to offer her is more floors to scrub."

"You still don't understand, do you? Maybe you can't. I want her to stand on her own two feet. Let her decide then what she wants. And if that doesn't include me . . ." I can feel my voice grow thicker with tears. First confiding in this woman, now crying in front of her. "My mother would have said that love is when you want what's best for the other person, even if you don't get to be the one who gives it to them."

Her face isn't just crumpling now. It's more like entire walls coming down. I feel a sharp twist of pity for her, this mother who in her own tortured way thought she was doing the best she could. Now she uses her silk sleeve to wipe her face clean. Back to normal, back under control.

I have three minutes left. The thoughts I'm trying to form are just images: me trying and failing to wrestle the knife away. Or succeeding, with a weapon in my hand I don't want to use on this woman, monster or not.

"What are you going to do with that thing, Mrs. Miramontes?"

"You know, dear, I think at this point you can just call me Inés. And what I'm going to do is order you to get the hell away from me now and go into my daughter's room and shut the door." She says this with the knife back up at my ribs, steady and sure. Except that her eyes are anything but. I have to walk away from those eyes, and Violeta's door shutting behind me is like a thunderclap. I sit next to Violeta's bed, where we can both hear the key turning, the door opening wide. And then nothing at all.

The watch on my wrist ticks out a minute. Two. And then the doorknob turns.

Mrs. Miramontes is standing in the door in her blue nightgown, looking for all the world like Judith after she slayed Holofernes, except that the thing hanging from the end of her hand is a bracelet, smeared in blood. She never had much color to her face, but now every bit of it is blanched and gone, and for a second I wonder if I've unleashed some other spell, and brought a ghost to the door. Then she settles the bracelet into my palm.

"You were asleep, weren't you, Nati?" Mrs. Miramontes tells

me, and she's shaking so badly that I want to cover her with every quilt in the house. But I can't move. "You stayed up late last night reading that book"—she points to the copy of *Rebecca*, the one camouflaging *Malcolm X*—"and so after checking on my daughter this morning, you found yourself having fallen asleep by her bed."

I can only nod, feeling the bloody metal weighing down my hand.

"Good. And therefore you certainly didn't hear or see anything. Not until I knocked on your door to tell you the terrible news." Then she crosses the hallway to Andrés's study, and I can hear it opening with the skeleton key, and she says the next words loud enough that I can hear her through the wall.

"Operator, please get the police. Something horrible's happened. I've just killed my son-in-law."

After she hangs up, she stands again in the doorway, clutching the wood.

"Do you think you could give me a few minutes alone with my daughter?" She gestures at Violeta, eyes staring at her mother's splattered hands. "Before the police arrive?"

I stay outside the door, so I can see Mrs. Miramontes as she leans over Violeta, looking into her wide black eyes. "Can you ever forgive me?" is all she says, and I know I should turn away and give them this moment alone, but I have to see the answer. There's a long moment when there's nothing at all, nothing but the sirens beginning to call, reaching a higher and higher pitch. Violeta's eyes are fixed on her mother for so long I think she's not going to respond. Then they slowly blink, once, and then nothing else. I translate for her. *Yes.*

Then Mrs. Miramontes clutches the doorway, her head hanging heavy and low. And the knock sounds on the door, and she heads down to meet the police, hands empty, peignoir smearing blood down the stairs.

They believe her, of course. It's a story woven so tightly and well: a woman descending into madness, raving about devils and silver mines ("aging woman," I caught one of the detectives writing in his little notebook), and convinced that her son-in-law was the devil and could only be conquered by blood. The cops have no reason to search the little maid's closet for a doll in a stained blue dress, or a tin that once held Mother's Cookies, painted in black.

All morning, the flow doesn't let up. Cops and photographers, a reporter or two. When Fernanda arrives she stands in the hallway, her face entirely inscrutable, as the cops fill her in. I catch her eye from the top of the stairs, and the second the cops look away I see the tiny corners of her mouth turn up, and she nods at me, the look in her eyes seeming to say, *Well done.* Then she turns away, quick and neat. I make a mental note to take down her home address, so that in a few months she might find a mysterious envelope in her mailbox, with bills from the family's petty cash. I might have done all this much faster if I'd found a way to team up with her. *I could have told you that,* my mother would have said.

It's early afternoon before I'm finally left alone with Violeta.

The picture is thawed, the trap unsprung, the bloodied bracelet put on her wrist, where I can slice it right off. The men on the record player sing their backward tune, maybe deciding they no longer want a paper doll, maybe deciding on a real companion instead, one that they can never control. They'll have to count on being good enough, and on loving her well enough, that she'll choose to stay by their side.

A sound comes from Violeta's throat. It sounds exactly like what it is: muscles kept asleep for six years, fighting to summon a hint of their old strength, to remember the moves they used to make. They finally form one syllable, then another, as I clasp her hands, and I feel them move under mine.

"Nati."

TWENTY-ONE

My dear Nati,

Please forgive me that this message is so short. Writing is still very slow, and painful. The nurse offered to have me dictate this, but I refused. The doctors here say I have recovered a lot of muscle tone, but they also warn me that I may never get back everything I lost.

I still don't forgive my mother. I meant it when I said that I could. But I try every day and I still don't. The best I can do is to hope to someday understand. I send her pictures of my recovery, like the one I am sending you. Don't be scared of the crutches. Someday they will be a cane, and someday I will stand entirely on my own two feet. Thanks, always and forever, to you.

I hope you understand why I haven't written before now. I think of you every day. I asked the staff to bring me every Nina Simone and Otis Redding album there is, and they smiled but agreed. This place is the best that money can buy, after all, and as Andrés's next of kin I have plenty.

The house and the land have been sold. You will get a letter from a law firm, and a check. I know you might refuse it. That's your right, though I hope you won't. I can't hope to repay you. Not ever.

They keep asking me what I will do when I am strong enough to leave. My answer is always the same: I have no clue. I don't have to decide anytime soon. I love to choose all the little things—pudding or ice cream for dessert, which hallway to walk down, which songs to play and replay—but anything larger than that terrifies me. All I want is to feel my body grow a little bit stronger each day, and to look out the window and think of you, and the last time I saw you, before the taxi pulled up to bring me here. You kept one bracelet. I kept its twin. The first choice I made, the first time in my life I was ever fully free. Thanks, always and forever, to you.

Oh, Nati. What signature could I possibly give?

Violeta

TWENTY-TWO

It's a bright, warm day in July, and I'm reading the letter again. I keep her letters in a painted wooden box, although mostly what she sends are postcards, tucked in with pictures. Violeta sitting up in a chair, unassisted; leaning on a walker, her shoes pointing their way out the door. Violeta reading *The Autobiography of Malcolm X*.

This letter has begun to split at the creases, I've read it so many times. "Nati, why not just call her?" asked Doris one night, when she found me on the sofa, wiping away tears.

"Because I'm letting her call me. When we said goodbye, I told her that she's spent so many years choosing nothing. I want her to remember what it feels like to decide things. And I don't want her to do anything because she feels like she owes me. Not even pick up the phone. I want it to be for real."

There's also a thick envelope in the box: a registered letter, from a firm called Hawkins and Stone, and a check. The money is everything I wanted, back when I started this. Now every time I pick it up, I imagine daiquiris on the beach, the sun on my back . . . but, also, the weight of that millstone, how it warped Violeta's mother. Her grandfather. Everybody it touched. *You're a good person, Natalia. Don't you want to stay that way?* And then there's my nagging doubt, that maybe the money was Violeta's way of saying goodbye.

So the check stays, ignored. I've picked up the pieces of my life right where I left them, hoping they'd still fit. And they have. Sort of, mostly. The phone has stayed silent, and I try to tell myself that maybe this is her answer, and that I can learn to accept it. I have to, if I meant at all what I said.

It's my turn to clean up after dinner, so I shove the letter back in its box. It keeps company with the Mother's Cookies tin, right out on the dresser where it catches the afternoon light. There's no point pretending that shoving the tin in a closet will stop me from opening it up again someday, any more than throwing it into a creek bed ever did. I pick up Grandma's earrings, the light winking off the gold squares. It's been weeks and I haven't needed to use them: I haven't felt any strange fingers running along my spine or any sudden, inexplicable chills. I guess Grandma decided she'd do best to leave me alone. I know I've decided that about her. I run my hands over the slips of paper I used for the dancing spell. Maybe sometime I'll amuse Doris and Lupe, or whoever the newest couch girl is, if I can lure enough moths.

Our neighbors are gone for the weekend, so I turn up the kitchen radio as loud as I want, and Lupe and I sing along with Stevie Wonder while we put the dishes away. Doris goes to answer the door; Andrea's coming over to watch *Laugh-In.* She promised to bring the wine.

"Nati? There's someone here for you."

Everything is in slow motion: the steam curling into the air from the sink full of hot water, Stevie's voice from the radio, my feet moving me to the stairwell, where Violeta is standing in a burgundy dress, leaning on a cane.

Doris heads back to the kitchen, and I hear the apartment door shut behind me. Now it's just me and Violeta in the echoing stairwell and I don't know where to look, what to do with my hands. Violeta's voice is low and cautious, still gathering strength.

"I still want to forgive my mother. I keep reminding myself how it was hard enough for me, growing up in that house, and I try to imagine what it must have been like for her. The chances she missed, to really know what love was like. And then she sacrificed herself so that I could know it. Because she knew that if you went into that room, Nati, there's no way it wouldn't have meant jail. Anywhere from assault to murder."

"I wasn't going to kill him. I wouldn't have gone that far." I'm pretty sure of that, anyway.

"Well, I would have."

I believe her. There's a beat of silence, and I try to keep my eyes from lingering on her mouth, those lips that I'm aching to brush with the tips of my fingers. That's the real reason why I haven't found some beach to lie on, drinking mai tais. It's because I want her in the lounge chair next to me.

"I rented an apartment. I made sure it was near here. I still can't walk for very long. There's so much I can't offer you, Nati. So much I don't know, except . . . I know I've never stopped wanting you. So if you'll still have me—"

And then I can't stand it anymore. I cross the distance between us and wrap my hands around her waist, and I murmur, my lips next to hers, "Can I kiss you?" and of course the answer is *yes.* And this, here, is our first kiss. The first she's given for no other reason than she wants to.

We start tender, and soft, but in her mouth I can feel the hunger that clawed inside me all through my teenage years, the hunger that howled when I swallowed that potion, that warmed and softened inside me the first time I saw two women reach for each other, without shame. She tastes like peppermint and lipstick and I reach for her breast, and I can feel it under my hand, that darkness that recognized itself, the twin to my own, and her heart actually flutters, as if leaping to meet my hand. "This is what it could be like," I quote to her, from her own words, and what comes from her mouth is both a gasp and a laugh. I kiss her throat, so she'll make that sound again, and now I have to drink from her lips, sweet and strong.

The apartment door opens. It's Lupe and Doris, purses on their shoulders, giggling, squeezing past us both.

"We decided to meet Andrea at the movies. There's a double feature at the Grand Lake. Don't expect us home before midnight," Doris calls to me, grinning, as they both thump down the stairs. She winks at Violeta before stepping outside. "Congratulations."

And Violeta blushes and reaches for my hand, and I help her healing body step over the threshold, and I can feel it in my hands as they pull her to me, that sweet rush of power that's been waiting for me all my life. A power I called up so I could do some good, help this damsel I'm holding now in my arms. And I can feel it humming in my chest, the song I'd once known but forgot, and it swells inside me, inside both of us, as I kiss her, and now I know it, I know the song.

AUTHOR'S NOTE

The Del Valle/Miramontes family is not based on any real family, at least as far as I know. I didn't want to use any one real family as a model, which meant not setting the action in Oakland. (All of Oakland is encompassed in what was a single land grant, to Luís María Peralta.) I instead picked Orinda, a nearby town that was home to several small-to-medium-size land grants, such as the one given to the fictional Mariano Vásquez Del Valle. None of the Orinda grantee families was a model, either; in fact, I deliberately avoided learning about those real families or their history, to avoid even inadvertently borrowing from the lives of real people with real descendants.

While the Miramontes family is an invention, the history of land theft and land loss after the Mexican-American War (1846–1848) is not. That war, which the United States launched on a fabricated pretext, allowed the US to steal huge swaths of Mexican land, including the province known then as Alta California. And the hundreds of thousands of Californios (Spanish and mixed-race people who'd already been living there) found their status radically changed overnight. To take just one example: The California Land Act of 1851 officially rendered all pre-1848 land grants "public domain and available for resettlement" until landholders could prove the legitimacy of their land rights. And because the courts often rejected land grants and deed documents that weren't written in English, this act paved the way for massive legalized theft. There were instances in which landholders had to fight all the way to the Supreme Court for restoration of their property.

In many ways, the seed of this book came from a document that I read in an exhibit at the Oakland Museum of California; it was an excerpt of a speech given in 1857 by a prominent Californio advocate and state senator, Pablo de la Guerra, to the California State Senate, on behalf of these landholders: "I have seen old people, sixty and seventy years old, crying like children because they had been cast out from the hearth of their ancestors. . . . They are the conquered kneeling before the conqueror, pleading to be protected in the enjoyment of the little that their hard fortune had left them." I was utterly struck by both the injustice and rank racism that de la Guerra was describing, and by his stunning lack of irony. (Just who had conquered whom, exactly, in order to create the province of Alta California in the first place?) These former Spanish and colonial land-grant holders had apparently been fine with a system of racial hierarchy, as long as they ended up on the top.

These contradictions stayed with me when I was outlining *Muñeca*, and they deeply informed how I wrote the Miramontes family. I wanted to anchor the story in a family carrying a heavy weight of loss and nostalgia for the glory days of their past, and a deep distrust of the social and political changes that the present had brought. So it made sense to invent a family with that kind of backstory, and to set it in the spring of 1968, when liberation movements were sweeping the world.

I enjoyed weaving many real places into this story, although I did fudge some dates. Sweet's Ballroom, popular among Black and Latine residents, seems to have closed in the mid-1960s, before Violeta and Doris and Andrea went dancing there. (I have also shamelessly invented a Screamin' Jay Hawkins concert happening there in the mid-1950s.) And as far as I know, the Jubilee, a venerable semiunderground lesbian bar in East Oakland, was not yet open in 1965, when Nati began meeting women there; the earliest listing I can find has it being open in 1969. (I did find evidence of three Oakland queer clubs that were in operation in the 1950s, because police carried out arrests there for "sexual deviance": Pearl's, the Hilltop Bar, and the Occidental.) The only queer club in Oakland that I could positively identify as having existed in 1968 was the White Horse, near the Berkeley border; it is said to be the oldest continuously running queer bar in the US. But I decided that a house party was the kind of space where my characters, and their found family, spent more of their time.

The house party in *Muñeca*'s introductory chapter owes its existence to a picture I found in the book *Wide-Open Town*, by Nan Alamilla Boyd, of a party from 1968. These parties were an alternate space where queer women of color could gather and meet even if they felt unwelcome at existing white-dominated queer bars or weren't as comfortable going to more public places. I decided that these parties might well have been happening as far back as 1965. *Wide-Open Town* is an excellent book on the history of Bay Area queer nightlife before Stonewall; its focus is San Francisco but the book still provides an invaluable understanding and helps to show just how deep and broad the Bay Area queer nightlife scene was at that time. In addition to Boyd's book, I also recommend *East Bay Yesterday*'s interview with Bay Area Lesbian Archives' founder Lenn Keller, as well as the archives from the Bay Area GLBT Historical Society Museum.

A few other notes on the historical background of this story: In 1962, when Violeta wanted to divorce Andrés, there was no state in the US that permitted no-fault divorce. This meant that Violeta would have had to convince a judge that Andrés had committed fraud (against Violeta herself), bigamy, violence, or infidelity, before she could be released from her marriage. California was the first US state to pass a law allowing for no-fault divorce—seven years later, in 1969. And it was not until 1974 that homosexuality was removed from the *Diagnostic and Statistical Manual of Mental Disorders*, declassifying it as grounds for involuntary hospitalization. The threat of being institutionalized had hung over women of Mrs. Miramontes's generation for their entire lives; by the mid-1960s, that threat had begun to ease slightly, but it was not gone.

A note on naming inspirations: Nati's mother got her name from Jovita Idar, a Chicana journalist, activist, and suffragist active in Texas in the early 1900s. Andrés is named after Andrés Asencio, the ruthless and ambitious politician at the center of Ángeles Mastretta's novel *Arráncame la vida*, whose wife, Catalina "Cati" Guzmán, proves to be a formidable match for him. And, yes, Violeta is named after exactly who you think she is.

ACKNOWLEDGMENTS

I've said this before: Books have so many tiny midwives, and as I sit to write this I'm terrified I'll forget some of them. But here is my attempt, anyway.

The bulk of this book was shared, six pages at a time, with the San Francisco Writers Workshop in its online sessions; thank you to all the writers who shared their helpful feedback, week after week. T. K. Rex helped me flesh out elements of Mrs. Miramontes's character, and of the plot, that proved to be critical. Gordon B. White hosted (still hosts) regular writing sessions and helped me understand elements of inheritance and property law that informed Violeta's situation. N. J. Gallegos helped me with medical knowledge that I then tossed aside, because Violeta's condition follows magical rules, not medical ones. I am still grateful for the understanding. As always, any mistakes are mine. And thank you to Lezlie Kinyon, who organized the writers' retreat in coastal Oregon where I wrote so many of these pages. I will not forget those long green days by the ocean, watching the mist burn off the trees.

I won't speak for others, but this is absolutely true for me: Without a good editor, good writing doesn't exist. Thank you to my editor, Daphne Durham, first for falling in love with *Muñeca* and then for your insightful and helpful work in shaping her to be her best self, the version that you all have just read. I always looked forward to reading your editorial comments. To Eric Raglin for editing an early draft, for making key suggestions that got *Muñeca* in a shape for me to send it around, and to Lindsay King-Miller, for being such a passionate cheering section. Thank you, my friend.

Thank you to my agent, Lauren Bajek, for championing not just this work but the kind of writing I want to do and who I want to write it for. And for shepherding me through a daunting, exciting process that sometimes felt like I had walked onto a movie set. I look forward to working with you on many books to come.

And thank you, as always, to my family, who reads everything I write, since the time I was writing it in crayon. And for shaping me into the kind of person who wanted to, and who could, write this book.

And thank you, reader, for picking up this book. I hope you enjoyed the journey.

ABOUT THE AUTHOR

Cynthia Gómez is the author of the short story collection *The Nightmare Box and Other Stories*, as well as a Tin House and VONA alum whose short fiction has been published in *Fantasy Magazine*, *Strange Horizons*, *PseudoPod*, *Nightmare Magazine*, and numerous anthologies. She lives in Oakland, California.